The LORD of the RINGS SKETCHBOOK

ALAN LEE

The
LORD
of the
RINGS
SKETCHBOOK

ALAN LEE

HarperCollins*Publishers*

Also illustrated by Alan Lee:

CASTLES

FAERIES

THE MABINOGION

THE MOON'S REVENGE

BLACK SHIPS BEFORE TROY

THE WANDERINGS OF ODYSSEUS

THE LORD OF THE RINGS

THE HOBBIT

THE ART OF THE LORD OF THE RINGS

THE HOBBIT SKETCHBOOK

HarperCollins*Publishers*
1 London Bridge Street,
London SE1 9GF

HarperCollins*Publishers*
Macken House, 39/40 Mayor Street Upper,
Dublin 1 D01 C9W8, Ireland

www.tolkien.co.uk

Published by HarperCollins*Publishers* 2005

19

Copyright © Alan Lee 2005
Illustrations © Alan Lee 1991, 2005

Alan Lee asserts the moral right to be identified as the author of this work

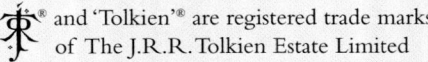 ® and 'Tolkien'® are registered trade marks
of The J.R.R. Tolkien Estate Limited

All sketches produced specifically during the development of *The Lord of the Rings*
film trilogy are reproduced courtesy of New Line Productions, Inc.

Editor: Chris Smith
Design: Gary Day-Ellison/www.day-ellison.com

ISBN 978 0 261 10383 2

Set in Trajan & Bembo

Printed and bound in India by Replika Press Pvt. Ltd.

All rights reserved. No part of this publication may be reproduced, stored in a retrieval system, or transmitted, in any form or by any means, electronic, mechanical, photocopying, recording or otherwise, without the prior permission of the publishers.

CONTENTS

FOREWORD	8
INTRODUCTION	10
CONCERNING HOBBITS	12
BARROWS AND BREE-LANDERS	33
RIVENDELL	44
MORIA	59
LOTHLÓRIEN	69
BORDERLANDS	79
ROHAN	84
FANGORN	87
EDORAS	93
HELM'S DEEP	101
THE ROAD TO MORDOR	109
ITHILIEN	118
MINAS TIRITH	132
THE ARMIES GATHER	144
THE BLOW FALLS	154
THE STEWARD'S TOMB	156
GROND	159
CIRITH UNGOL	168
MORDOR	176
THE GREY HAVENS	184
ACKNOWLEDGEMENTS	188

FOREWORD

When I met Peter Jackson and Fran Walsh in London, six months before they started shooting *The Lord of the Rings* in New Zealand, they enticed me by showing some startling pictures of Middle-earth. On two scores this was a clincher to the suggestion that I might play Gandalf. Marvelling at the spectacular designs, this was my introduction to a saga which I hadn't then read and more, a realisation that, although the enterprise of the two modest Kiwis was hugely ambitious, if the graphics were anything to go by it was also achievable.

I relished those designs even more when later I walked onto the sets that reproduced them in the Stone Street Studios in Wellington, as well as in the open-air locations all over the two main islands of New Zealand. It was like stepping into the pages of a storybook – almost literally, because of course the films' principal scenic inspiration came from Alan Lee and John Howe, whose work has illustrated Tolkien's words alongside the author's own designs.

It has not been often enough realised that when a reader recognises Tolkien's characters and their surroundings in the films as being "exactly how I'd always imagined", a mistake is being made. In truth, what is being recognised from the writing has been filtered through the lens of the pictures that accompany them. Not that there is anything photographic about Alan Lee's work. He is a master of the ancient arts of sketching and watercolouring and his notations in this book describe well how the artist's imagination has reached the page so confidently.

What a unique curiosity is in your hands! The Lee sketchbook feels and looks like other artists' records of great journeys to foreign lands. But in Alan Lee's case, his sketches of Middle-earth and its inhabitants preceded the travel, and the country he helped uncover in New Zealand was partly of his own making.

The Fellowship actors have often been asked whether the green-(or sometime blue-)screen technique of acting in front of a blank wall, on which later the scenery will be projected, is not a difficulty. For those of us who have worked onstage in front of castle battlements that are made of canvas, and stone that is merely painted wood, reality is the last thing that is expected in theatre settings and in films too. Yet in New Zealand, Middle-earth seemed complete, ready and waiting for crew and actors time and time again. One of my happiest days ever was spent thanks to a helicopter on the alps of the South Island, high above the snowline where the Fellowship climbed toward Moria.

Below us in the mighty arc of mountains was the plain where, until the interruption of the film-makers, only shepherds had ever visited. On top of a lone outcrop, perhaps a remnant of prehistoric ice movements along the valley, as drawn by Alan Lee, Edoras had been built. From the wrong side where the service road ran to the Golden Hall, it was not intended to film. So there the cables snaked and the builders had not bothered to decorate. On a film set, nothing is as it seems. Today all evidence of Rohan has been removed, as was the bargain, and the shepherds' plain is empty once more.

Edoras survives in the trilogy of films along with so much else of Alan Lee's imagination. But here there is still more – an insight into an artist's mind and a close-up of his pen, pencil and brushes at work. Wonderful.

Ian McKellen

Ian McKellen

London 2005

INTRODUCTION

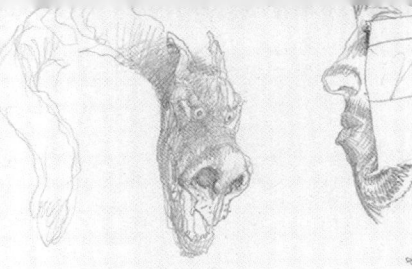

I first read *The Lord of the Rings* when I was seventeen, and working as a gardener in a cemetery. Every day I would lose myself among the ivy-covered crypts and shadowy groves, and in the evenings immerse myself in the strange and beautiful world that J. R. R. Tolkien's books had opened up for me. I had loved myths and legends from the moment that I first encountered them, and it felt as though everything in those stories that most appealed to me had been distilled and refined and forged into this totally compelling narrative. So the outer suburbs of Middlesex became Middle-earth, and my friends became Rangers, and I decided that I would really rather illustrate books than tend graves.

After studying graphics and illustration for three years, and another six earning a living doing paperback covers, my dream of being able to illustrate the stories

that I liked best started to bear fruit. There were books of fairy lore, and Celtic myths, and Arthurian stories, and eventually I found myself talking to Rayner Unwin and Jane Johnson about the idea of an illustrated edition of *The Lord of the Rings* to commemorate the centenary of its author's birth.

I was pleased to be offered the chance to illustrate one of my favourite books, but also a little daunted by the responsibility involved in placing my illustrations alongside a text that was so deeply loved by its many admirers, and which had already demonstrated that it worked very well on its own, without any pictures. I think the Tolkien Estate were even more nervous about it than I was, and I was asked to do some drawings of how the characters may be represented before they would give the go-ahead.

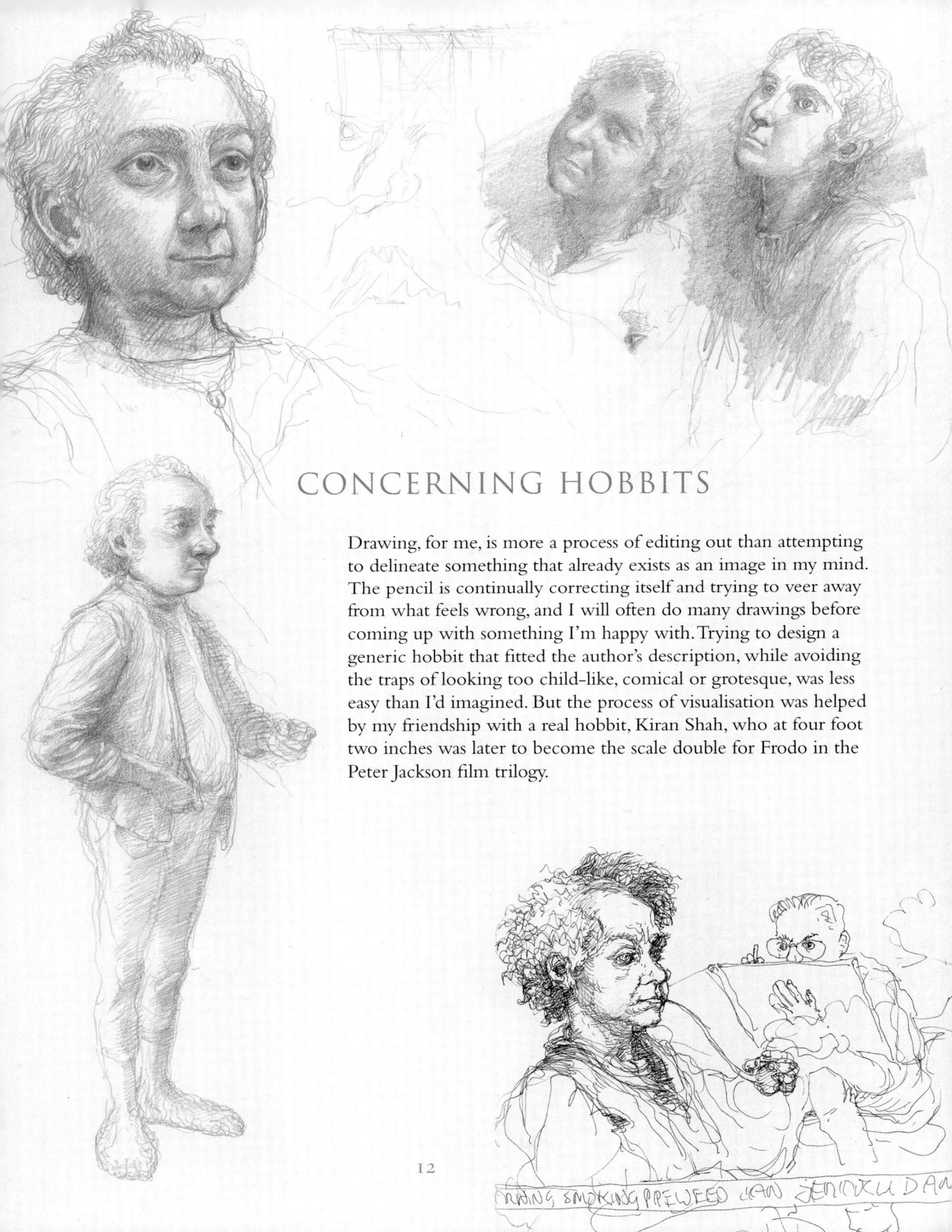

CONCERNING HOBBITS

Drawing, for me, is more a process of editing out than attempting to delineate something that already exists as an image in my mind. The pencil is continually correcting itself and trying to veer away from what feels wrong, and I will often do many drawings before coming up with something I'm happy with. Trying to design a generic hobbit that fitted the author's description, while avoiding the traps of looking too child-like, comical or grotesque, was less easy than I'd imagined. But the process of visualisation was helped by my friendship with a real hobbit, Kiran Shah, who at four foot two inches was later to become the scale double for Frodo in the Peter Jackson film trilogy.

Bilbo Baggins - esquire

When we first meet Frodo he is thirty-three, and just 'coming of age', though it is seventeen years later that his quest really begins. In my illustrations he looked quite a bit younger; being unsure of the rate at which hobbits mature, I kept him in a state of indeterminate youth, alongside Gandalf's indeterminate old age. Gandalf, as a Maia, is immortal, but he has inhabited his present body for around two thousand years.

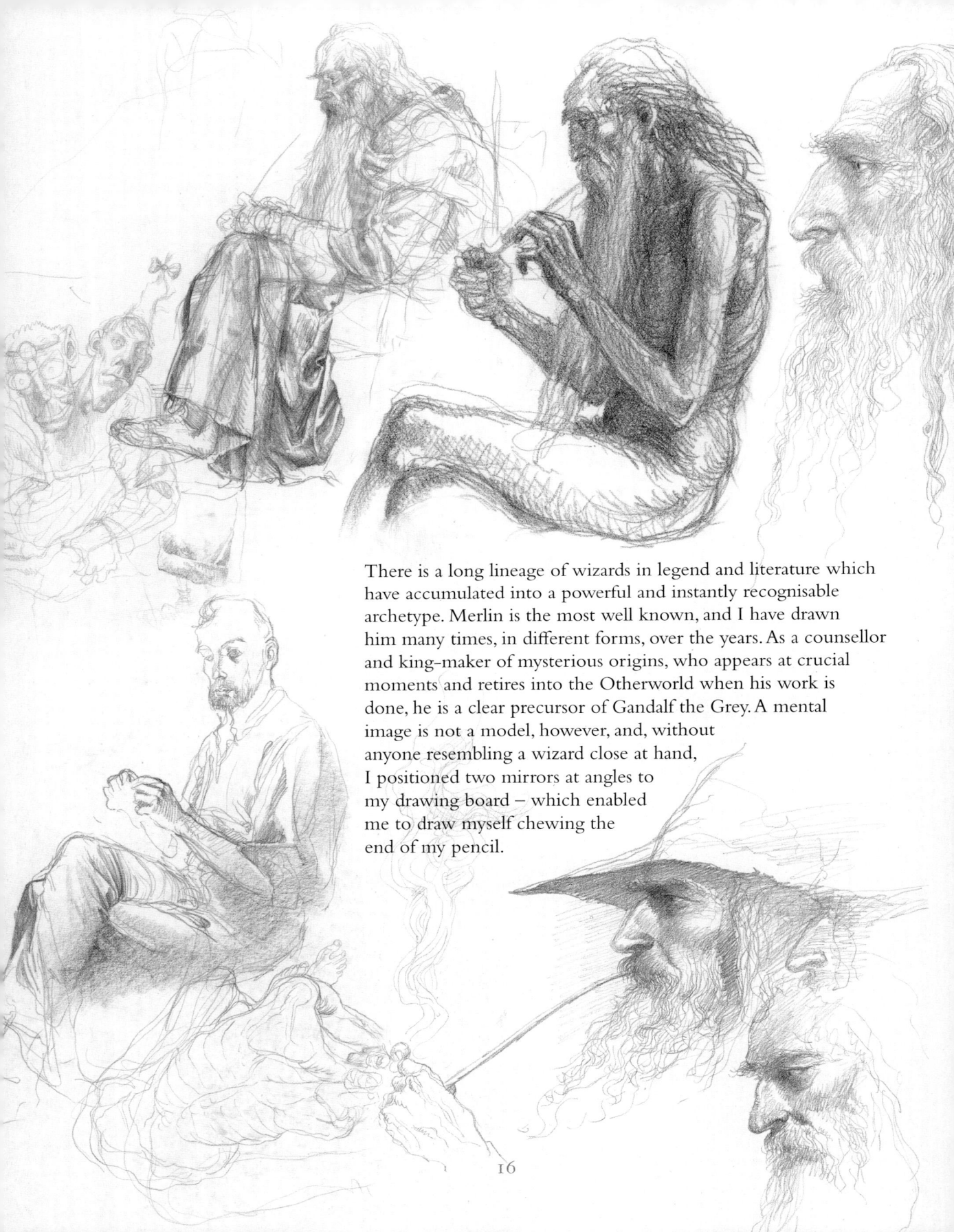

There is a long lineage of wizards in legend and literature which have accumulated into a powerful and instantly recognisable archetype. Merlin is the most well known, and I have drawn him many times, in different forms, over the years. As a counsellor and king-maker of mysterious origins, who appears at crucial moments and retires into the Otherworld when his work is done, he is a clear precursor of Gandalf the Grey. A mental image is not a model, however, and, without anyone resembling a wizard close at hand, I positioned two mirrors at angles to my drawing board – which enabled me to draw myself chewing the end of my pencil.

One of the first things I do when I start to illustrate a book is to create a page plan, so that I have an overview of what I have to do. Then I can begin by thinking of the shape and dynamics of the whole thing before getting involved with the detail of any one individual picture. This initial plan, which I'll try to fit onto one sheet of paper, or one page in a sketchbook, will consist of tiny, roughly drawn thumbnails, which change and get moved about as the book develops. It helps to make a project seem manageable if there is some visual representation, however half-baked, of the finished result. Lists don't work for me. If I have something to organise, like packing for a trip, I'll draw an open suitcase, with tiny images of everything that I'll need stacked around it, before starting to collect the real objects.

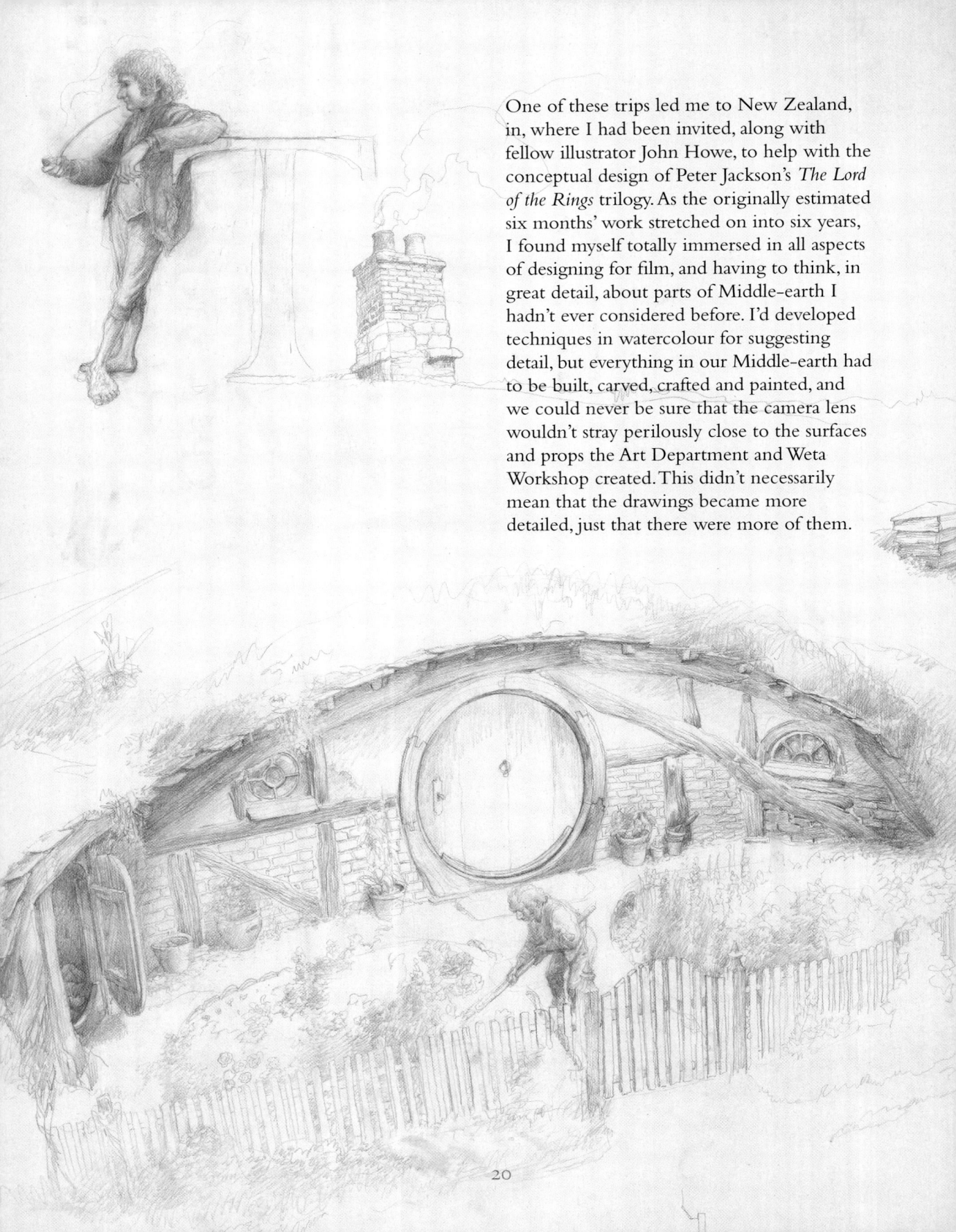

One of these trips led me to New Zealand, in, where I had been invited, along with fellow illustrator John Howe, to help with the conceptual design of Peter Jackson's *The Lord of the Rings* trilogy. As the originally estimated six months' work stretched on into six years, I found myself totally immersed in all aspects of designing for film, and having to think, in great detail, about parts of Middle-earth I hadn't ever considered before. I'd developed techniques in watercolour for suggesting detail, but everything in our Middle-earth had to be built, carved, crafted and painted, and we could never be sure that the camera lens wouldn't stray perilously close to the surfaces and props the Art Department and Weta Workshop created. This didn't necessarily mean that the drawings became more detailed, just that there were more of them.

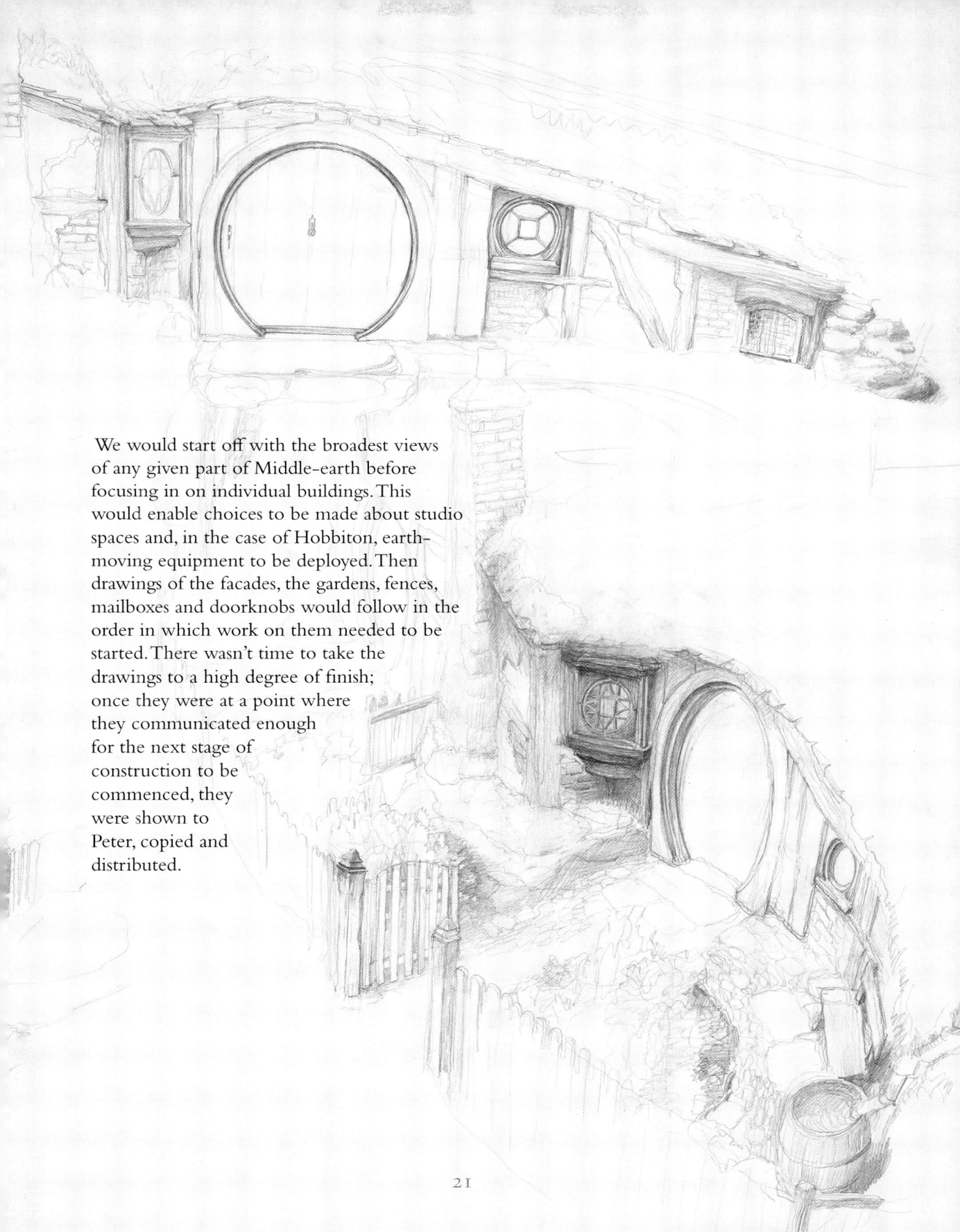

We would start off with the broadest views of any given part of Middle-earth before focusing in on individual buildings. This would enable choices to be made about studio spaces and, in the case of Hobbiton, earth-moving equipment to be deployed. Then drawings of the facades, the gardens, fences, mailboxes and doorknobs would follow in the order in which work on them needed to be started. There wasn't time to take the drawings to a high degree of finish; once they were at a point where they communicated enough for the next stage of construction to be commenced, they were shown to Peter, copied and distributed.

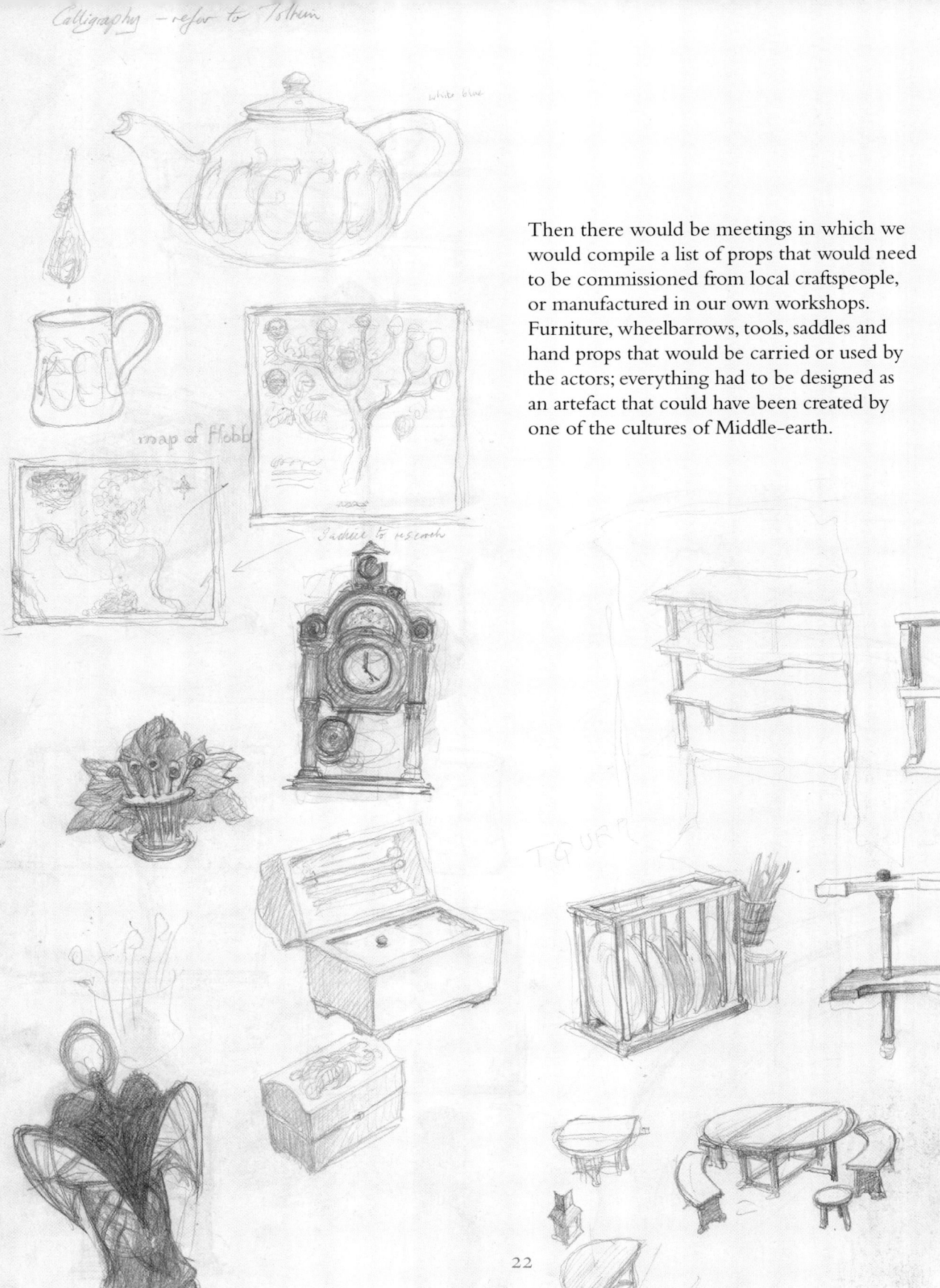

Then there would be meetings in which we would compile a list of props that would need to be commissioned from local craftspeople, or manufactured in our own workshops. Furniture, wheelbarrows, tools, saddles and hand props that would be carried or used by the actors; everything had to be designed as an artefact that could have been created by one of the cultures of Middle-earth.

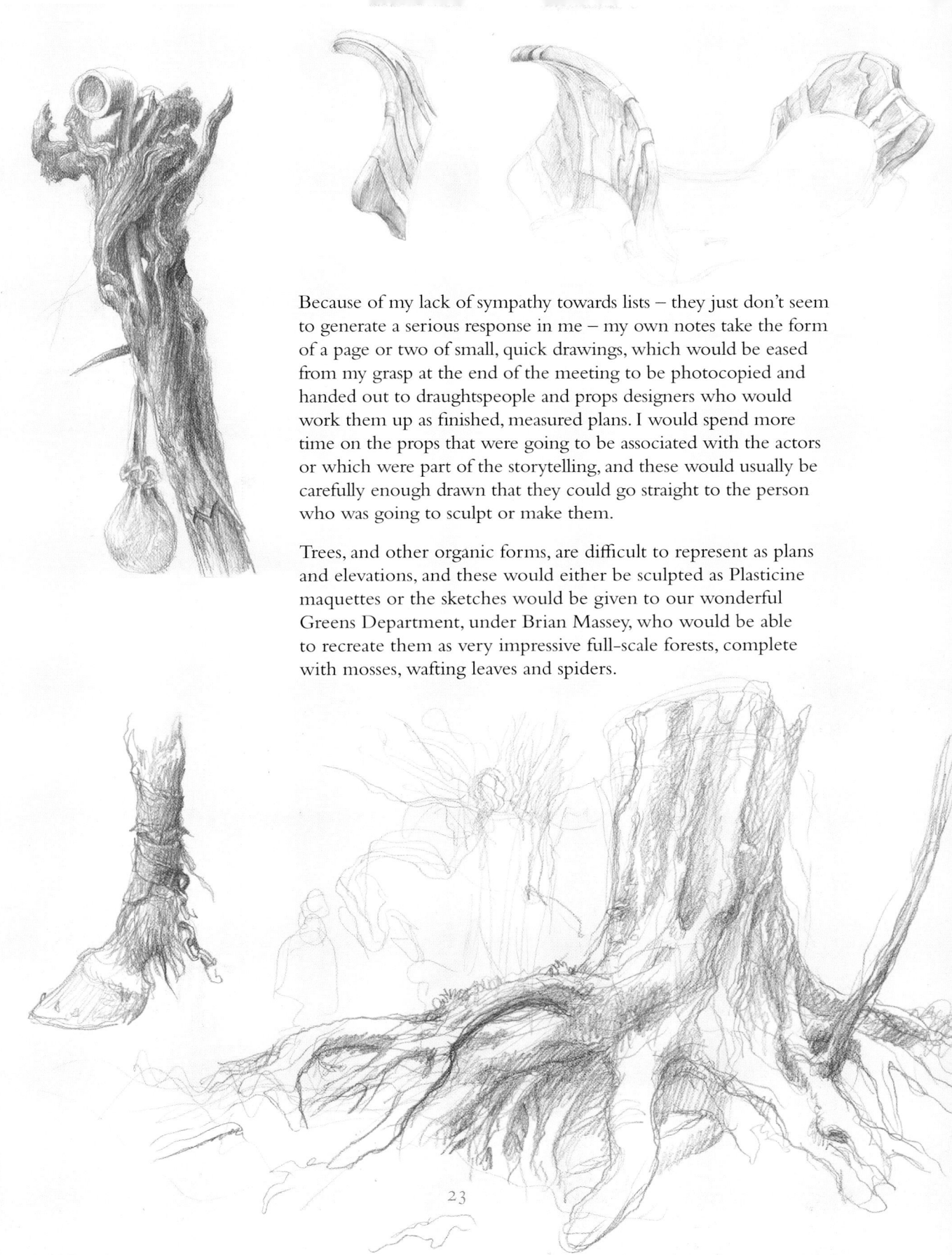

Because of my lack of sympathy towards lists – they just don't seem to generate a serious response in me – my own notes take the form of a page or two of small, quick drawings, which would be eased from my grasp at the end of the meeting to be photocopied and handed out to draughtspeople and props designers who would work them up as finished, measured plans. I would spend more time on the props that were going to be associated with the actors or which were part of the storytelling, and these would usually be carefully enough drawn that they could go straight to the person who was going to sculpt or make them.

Trees, and other organic forms, are difficult to represent as plans and elevations, and these would either be sculpted as Plasticine maquettes or the sketches would be given to our wonderful Greens Department, under Brian Massey, who would be able to recreate them as very impressive full-scale forests, complete with mosses, wafting leaves and spiders.

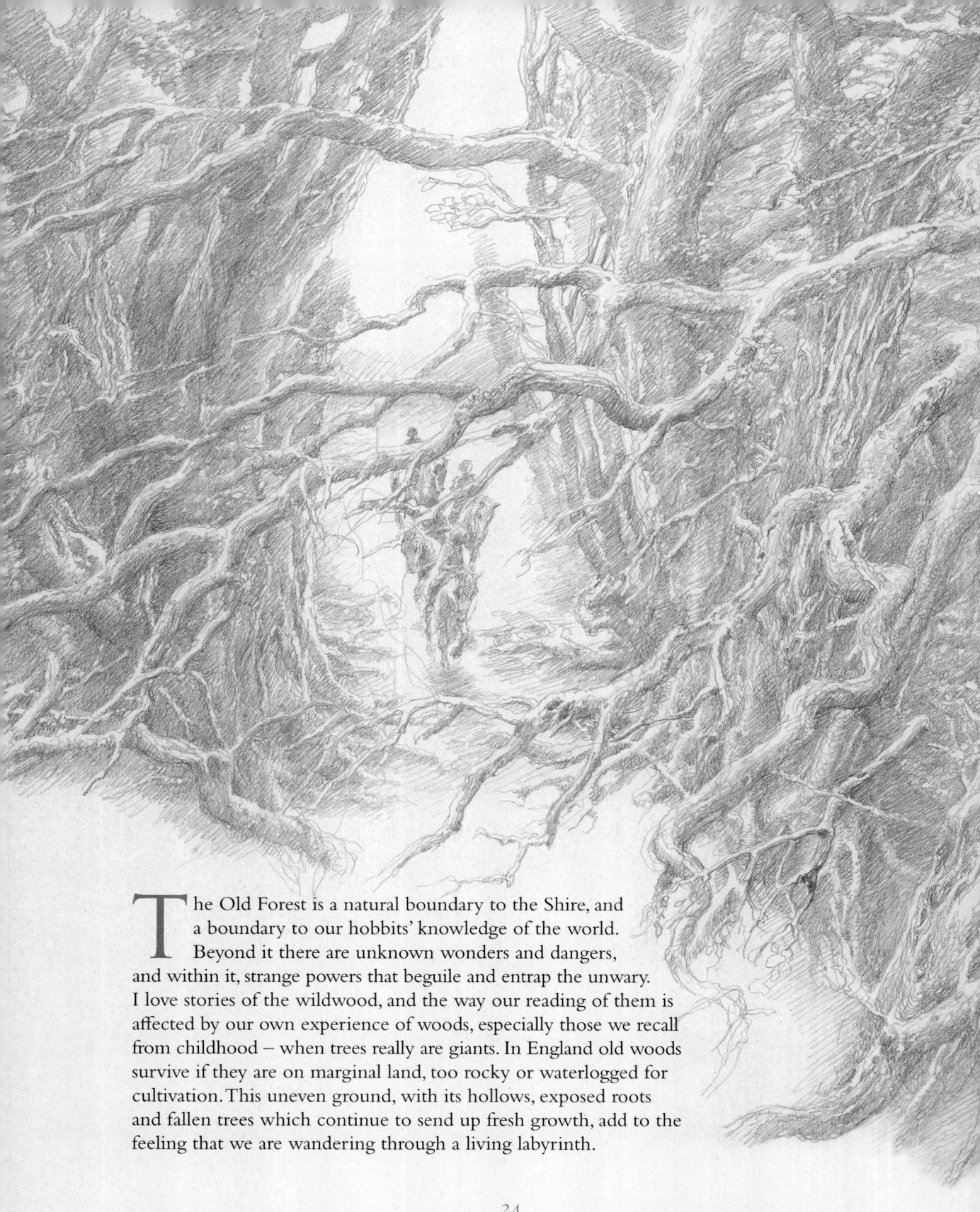

The Old Forest is a natural boundary to the Shire, and a boundary to our hobbits' knowledge of the world. Beyond it there are unknown wonders and dangers, and within it, strange powers that beguile and entrap the unwary. I love stories of the wildwood, and the way our reading of them is affected by our own experience of woods, especially those we recall from childhood – when trees really are giants. In England old woods survive if they are on marginal land, too rocky or waterlogged for cultivation. This uneven ground, with its hollows, exposed roots and fallen trees which continue to send up fresh growth, add to the feeling that we are wandering through a living labyrinth.

Our first encounter with one of the few malevolent inhabitants of the wildwood – Old Man Willow – is followed, just in time, by the arrival of Tom Bombadil, one of Tolkien's odder creations. Outlandishly dressed, and speaking in rhyme, he is a nature spirit, an embodiment and master of the land. He is a sort of Green Man, though it is songs and verse that spill from his mouth rather than vines and leaves. As in much of our heritage of folksong, among the 'merry dols' and 'ring a ding dillos' there are echoes of more potent and archaic tales – like the face of a powerful god peering through a mask of convoluted greenery.

I'm reminded of some of our old local folksingers when I think of Tom Bombadil, and so I've put him and Goldberry into a Devonshire longhouse. This isn't one building in particular; it is composed of elements from several houses that I'd sketched separately.

Barrows and Bree-landers

I live in an area rich in prehistoric burial mounds, stone circles and menhirs, so the pictures that arise in my mind when reading the barrow-wight episode are strongly reminiscent of Dartmoor. There have also been occasions when I've been completely disorientated by sudden fogs while walking on the moor. The skylarks and sunlit heather-clad hills disappear, to be replaced by boggy pools and the odd spectral sheep. The grip you think you have on reality is surprisingly tenuous when your world has been covered by a blanket of vapour, and the ground you are standing on is quaking like a turf-covered waterbed.

The best-preserved and most impressive Neolithic remains I have visited are on the island of Orkney, just off the northern tip of Scotland. Maes Howe, five thousand years old, is a beautifully constructed chambered tomb. In the Orkneyinga saga there is an account of how a group of Vikings, attempting to seize control of the islands, were forced to shelter there overnight during a blizzard, and how two of them were driven insane. Other Viking plunderers stayed long enough to carve runic inscriptions into the stone walls, so the wights may not have been permanent residents.

Though picturesque, Bree has a slightly dangerous and outlandish flavour. It is populated by a mixture of hobbits, dwarves and men, and there are transient and dubious characters in the streets and inns. It has something of the quality of the Wild West, where the saloon – the dark heart of the town – becomes the arena for sudden dramas and life-changing encounters. Our Bree was built in a military camp a few minutes' drive from the studio. The warped, half-timbered houses were constructed on top of the buildings that were already there, and you could step out of the muddy streets, through a medieval doorway, and into offices and barracks.

The actors would, of course, be stepping into other interior sets, built in the studios. We always had to bear in mind the scale issues: that our hobbits would need to be filmed in an oversized set with matching furniture and props – and extras – while everyone else needed a normal-sized environment. This meant that most of our sets, apart from those such as Bag End which required two environments identical in everything but size, had to be able to accommodate both scales in a small crowded studio. There were a number of ingenious and highly technical methods for maintaining these illusions, and these were very carefully applied, until Peter realised that once the audience were used to the idea that a good number of the cast were around three foot six inches tall, a lot could be achieved through simple, sleight of hand in-camera techniques, like getting actors to perform on their knees.

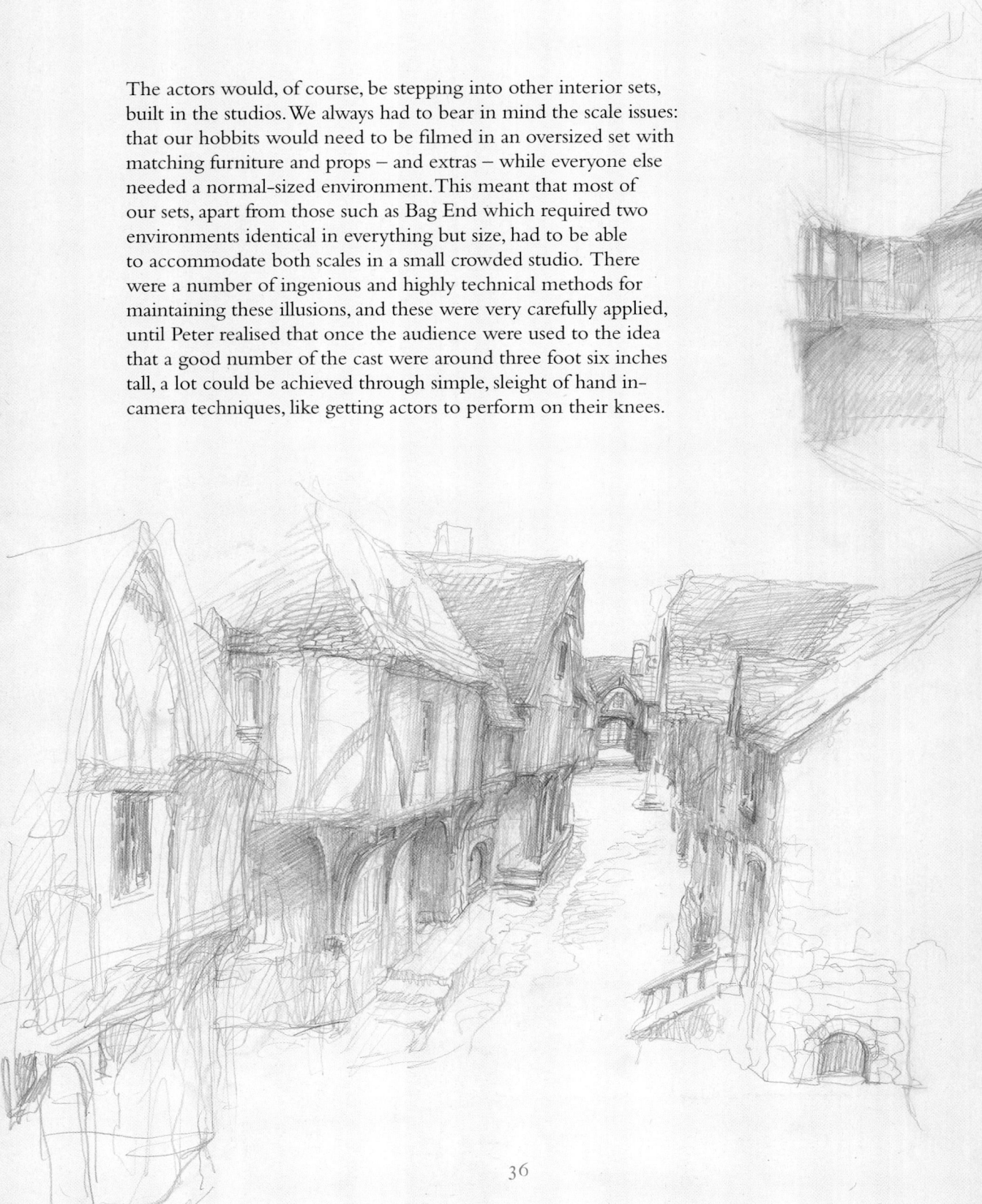

For the Weathertop ruins we had two sets, both built at human scale, with one oversized element – the fallen statue that Frodo cowers under as the Witch-king hunts him down. The dramatic and highly effective final look of the Ringwraiths was a combination of the work of Weta's skilled weapons- and armour-makers, following John Howe's initial drawings, and Ngila Dickson's brilliant costume design. Each of the wraiths was shrouded with around fifty metres of elegantly funereal material, distressed and tattered and designed to flow sinuously in the wind. My contributions to these scenes were drawings for the sets, and set dressing with Grant Major. This was very early in the shoot – the Weathertop fight scene was Viggo's first day on set as Aragorn – and I think I over-compensated with the detailing, wedging lumps of moss I'd picked out of brickwork in the street between our fake paving slabs, and planting dried grasses, stalk by stalk, into the areas that I thought the camera might get close to. This was one of the sets that were built as weather cover – which meant that it had to be ready for use at a moment's notice, but might remain almost complete and poised for action for several weeks. Every day Grant and I would look at the set and see some little detail that could be improved, and since the Greens Department invariably had about ten other huge sets in hand we would usually just do it ourselves.

Another contribution was the design of the crowns that the Nazgûl are wearing when we see them through Frodo's eyes in Wraithworld. The drawings on this page were done before Richard Taylor's designers at Weta – Jamie Beswarick and Mike Asquith in particular – had made models for the prosthetic faces that the very tall actors would be wearing. The final results were so striking that it would have been a pity to have obscured so much of their distorted features and corpse-like skin, and I did some lighter designs which were made up by Tony Drawbridge and Chris Streeter at the Art Department props workshop.

In the book there are ten days of trekking over difficult terrain between Weathertop and the forest in which Bilbo Baggins and his Dwarf companions had narrowly escaped becoming Troll cuisine. The need to maintain momentum and dramatic tension in a film treatment means that a contraction of time is often necessary, but throughout the films we tried to add detail and visual references to aspects of the story that would not form part of the main thrust of the storytelling, yet which enhance our appreciation of it, and our sense of the scope and history of Middle-earth. So it was great that Peter wanted to have the stone-trolls as part of the background for the scenes following Frodo's wounding at Weathertop, even though there was no reference to them in the dialogue. Normally, as part of a set, it would have been the Art Department's job to create them, but Weta's designers – with Ben Wootten taking the lead – were keen to make the maquettes, and the final huge and lumpen figures were carved by its team of Miniature builders.

There was a great degree of co-operation between the different departments, all working at the most intense level over the extensive period of production. The Art Department, consisting of about 400 carpenters, builders, prop-makers, sculptors, greensmen and women, painters and a 'rock and foam' department, produced 350 sets for the shoot, and probably another fifty or so for the pick-ups for all three films. There were also saddlers, textile artists and a calligrapher, while a wide variety of different craftsmen and women were commissioned to produce specialist items, like Elven glassware and Hobbit pottery.

Weta Workshop had over 200 people manufacturing miniatures, weapons and armour, prosthetics, and the design of creatures and other effects, while Weta Digital had about the same number hidden away in dark rooms putting the final effects shots together. Then there were the Miniatures film crews, the Costume Department, Make-up, Stunts, Casting; a team responsible for training and supplying horses. Add to this the lighting riggers, the five separate film crews, Sound, Editing and Music, production and location managers, Catering – and the cast – and you have over 2,000 people all devoted to a single end result: the creation of this wonderful alternative reality from a script, a book and their brilliant writers. You see and hear the work of everyone involved on the screen, or sense their energy and their work ethic, and the huge number of hours worked – with the inevitable occasional blunders and frayed nerves – are all transformed by the peculiar alchemy of film, and the skill and vision of the director, into this wonderful experience which is, at heart, pure storytelling.

And beyond this immediate collaborative effort, there was also a wider support in the community and country – almost a collective will to help make these films possible, so the Government, the local authorities, the Maori iwi and the New Zealand Army were all more than willing to help in any way possible to make it easier for us.

Exit, pursued by wraiths.

RIVENDELL

Tolkien's maps and descriptions of Middle-earth have been invaluable in helping all the illustrators who have been drawn to his material as well as his general readers. A sort of unspoken consensus is established in which the overall topography, and the broader evocations of colour, the starkness of rocks or the lushness of forest become rooted in the mind, even though the finer details remain hazy. What I wanted to do with the book illustrations was support and embellish the readers' interpretations, rather than offer radically new ideas, and so the text is followed quite carefully in order that the protagonists' movements could be tracked across the surface of the pictures and into its distances. The satisfaction for me comes from the process of finding that initial composition, and then building up the atmosphere with successive washes of watercolour until the feelings evoked by the words, and those evoked by the image, start to merge. If these basic things work then the details, which are usually where the most invention occurs, will be less questioned and more convincing.

Because of the nature of film – the shape of the screen, the desire of the camera to keep moving and exploring – and the amount of time we spend in these environments, we were asked by Peter to create quite an extensive miniature for Rivendell. Once he was happy with the general layout and style of architecture, it was a matter of producing copious amounts of Elven detailing, often in the form of patterns that could be scanned and returned a couple of days later as laser-cut plastic. After a while, that Elven aesthetic could be summoned up on request, and without much thought, in between designs for Dwarven tombs and Gondorian palaces. In essence you could describe it as Art Nouveau, with all the 19th-century flourishes and excesses edited out, in a kind of Scandinavian Shangri-La.

Rivendell was not just the 'last homely house', it was also an Elven refuge, and a place where relics from more glorious periods of Middle-earth history could be safely stored. I had designed the Pietà-like statue where the shards of the broken sword Narsil could be displayed, but there was also a mention in the script of *The Fellowship of the Ring* of a series of tapestries or murals that would help the viewer to make the link with events in the film's prologue. I did designs for seven paintings showing important moments in the history of the Elves and painted two myself – the retreat of the Noldor from Eregion, and the confrontation between Isildur and Sauron.

More crucially, Rivendell is the place where the heroes of the story assemble, the issues are discussed and the Fellowship is formed, with Frodo accepting his role along with the many dangers he will face. And another vital character makes his first appearance, though only as a worrying report from one of the Wood-elves who have captured and then lost him – Gollum.

I quite frequently use the compositional device of combining two pictures, or two different aspects of one idea, into one illustration. In this case it seemed appropriate that Gollum should occupy most of the upper half of the painting, given that he is being discussed at that moment. So here he is a sort of big pictorial thought-bubble, literally hanging over their heads, chewing the remains of a bird he has just grabbed.

One of the most important roles in the films was that filled by the majestic mountains, rivers, valleys and forests of New Zealand itself. Tolkien's descriptions of the landscapes of Middle-earth are, for me, the most beautiful and powerfully evocative element in his writings, and the choice of locations was to become a vital aspect of the film-making process. In many cases the practical benefits of shooting close to, or in, the studios was a dominating factor, but a huge amount of all three films was shot in real landscapes, and those are the scenes that really establish the scale, drama and beauty of the fictional world that the protagonists are moving through. Peter was keen to add a sense of history to many of these pristine landscapes, and so the Art Department would 'dress-in' some old broken arches, carried around the country by truck for the purpose, or Weta would achieve an even more dramatic effect by adding digitally modelled ruins into helicopter shots.

It was also important that the digitally created landscapes that are a part of so many of the shots should belong to that same world; that we shouldn't relapse into fantasy just because anything is possible. The matte-painted and computer-modelled mountains should be as real as the filmed ones, and so gathering scenic photographs became a priority, both during shooting and in post-production. A special unit was set up to collect material – usually in the form of photographic 'tiles' – a whole vista, sometimes of 360 degrees, made up of dozens of photographs shot in a grid formation. These were used most effectively in the Rivendell, Isengard and Mordor sequences. In addition to this, the film units themselves would usually take tiles of locations, to be used as backgrounds for any shots which might later be inserted into the scenes they were filming, as well as any good dawn skies or waterfalls they happened to spot.

I was able to share the exhilarating experience of exploring most of the places we were going to film, as well as many more that were close to, but not quite, perfect for use in those breathtaking scenes. This initial period of looking for locations was a revelation, frequently repeated as we returned to watch the progress of set building and filming. We revisited some of those sites during post-production, sometimes with a posse of matte painters, released for a day from their computers and blinking in the unaccustomed sunlight.

The trip I recall most vividly was undertaken during post-production on *The Return of the King*. Craig Potton, an excellent New Zealand photographer, myself and Libby Hazell – who was co-ordinating the trip – spent two wonderful days in Alfie Speight's helicopter, shooting the tiles that would be used to create the Pelennor fields, the White Mountains, Dunharrow and a number of other environments, and exploring huge tracts of remote mountainous landscape collecting material for matte and texture painters and compositors. By this stage I had pretty much stopped using drawn or painted backgrounds in the visual effects artwork I was doing, instead using Photoshop to position the photographs and film stills that had been taken.

Richard Taylor's Miniatures department, led by John Baster and Mary MacLachlan produced around 80 beautifully crafted cities, buildings and environments at a variety of different scales. The architectural ones had a lot of design input, but those which were more organic could usually proceed fairly quickly from an initial sketch to a maquette and on to the finished object. The Pass of Caradhras scenes required a miniature, complete with icicles and avalanches, to which were added a digitally modelled Fellowship, a matte-painted distant mountainscape and digital flurries of snow. These wide shots of the storm were intercut with closer shots filmed in one of the studios.

The Miniatures film unit, led by Alex Funke, shot a huge amount of footage over an extended period, and the amazing results are responsible for a large part of our engagement with the films. In so many movies the establishing wide shots, the matte-painted or CG vistas, are inserted as sudden flourishes, intended to impress. Peter's approach is to give the miniature and other effects work the same kind of treatment that he gives to the live action, so that one will flow naturally into the other and the story is propelled along, rather than interrupted.

The miniatures, beautifully finished and dressed to camera by Paul Van Ommen and his team, are sometimes made long before they are filmed, or even storyboarded, and the shots and sequences are often developed as a result of their design and fabrication, and the close attention that Peter gives them throughout that process. Their physical presence will suggest ideas in the same way that a location or a dressed set will inspire a particular camera angle. Because of this the miniatures were usually very complete, and created so that they could be viewed from any position.

During the initial stages of pre-production, when John, Grant, Dan and I were based at Weta with Richard, there was a particular urgency to the process of getting work on the miniatures underway. With so much to do, and the fact that a lot of the work on sets and locations would be based on them, creating designs for the miniatures was a first step in establishing the look of the film, rather than, as is usually the case, being a part of the post-production process. So while John was put to work in his role as Sauron's architect, as well as armourer and beastmaster, I began work on Helm's Deep, Rivendell and Moria.

58

MORIA

While in *The Hobbit* J.R.R. Tolkien's Dwarves are fairly broadly drawn prototypes; their names borrowed from Old Norse poetry and their manners from fairytale, by the time they re-emerge in *The Lord of the Rings* they have acquired a venerable and complex history, and Moria, their ancient home, is a lost civilisation. I found the whole episode in the book quite terrifying on first reading it, and was reminded of the experience of being in a fairground ghost-house when I was very young – in pitch darkness, and imagining vast, echoing spook-filled halls and plunging depths, all in a space about the size of a shed.

I didn't imagine for a minute that Dwarves might live in a scaled-down environment; their love of artifice, and of grand gestures, suggests that they would want to build on an epic, even gigantic scale – and besides, they had a whole mountain to play with.

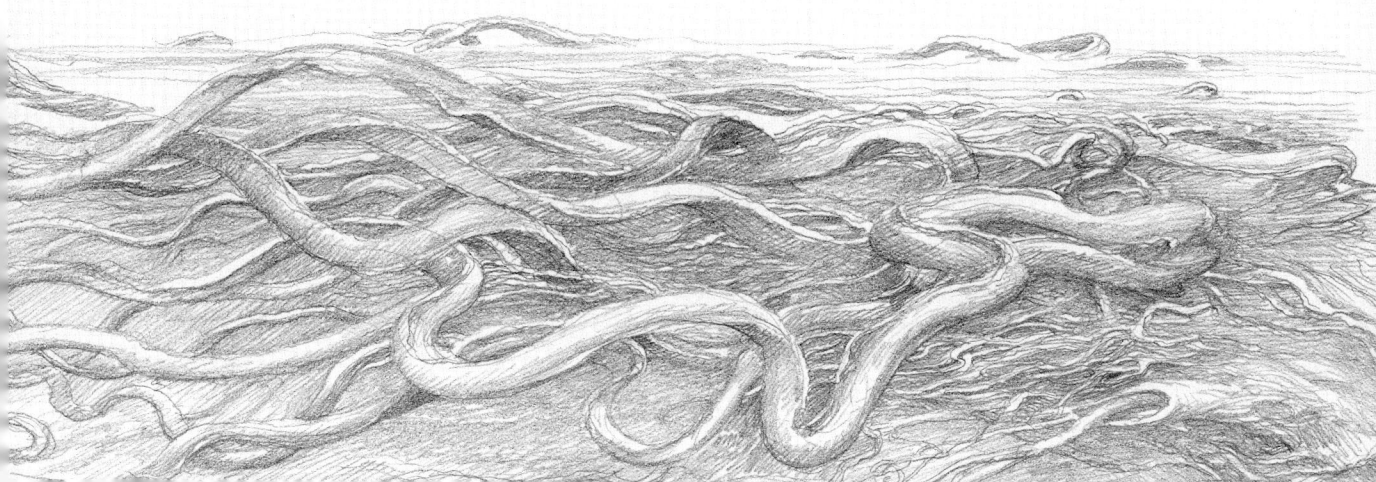

Pictures with a major architectural element need a highly structured perspective drawing as a framework. Once that's in place, I can take a more relaxed approach to working on the final watercolour, knowing that there is a strong foundation underpinning it. It can be a little frustrating to go through this process when you are itching to start splashing about in watercolour, but I have a strong memory of this pedantic old man who taught technical drawing in school, and was pretty dismissive of my efforts. I think I'm still trying to prove something to him.

We followed the Fellowship through the mountain step by step, drawing by drawing, miniature by miniature and set by set. We thought the architecture should have a geometric and crystalline quality – taking cues from the runes and gemstones that were so important to the Dwarves – and covered the walls of the Mazarbul chamber – the site of Balin's tomb – with pause-button-proof runic histories.

John has done many drawings and paintings of the Balrog, and these were the basis for further design work and some excellent sculpting by Ben Wootten. After their dramatic descent to the roots of the mountains, we thought that we might follow Gandalf and his fiery nemesis further; up the Endless Stair, with the Balrog becoming a creature of slime. I did a few drawings and Mary MacLachlan made some maquettes showing how that might look. Quite a lot of work was done by the Weta creature designers on what a slime Balrog might look like, but I think Peter decided that we might be pushing our luck, and the audience's pain threshold, by following their progress too closely.

The escape and exit from Moria was wonderfully recreated on film, with very moving performances, and these were amplified by the extraordinary, austerely beautiful scenery of Mount Owen. We had travelled there in one of our early location recces, looking for a cave, or a fold in the mountainside, where we could convincingly build a Dwarven back door. Though we hadn't found exactly what we were looking for, Peter liked the feel of the place and had the idea of building a digital extension to the mountain. A helicopter was used to get the wide shot, then the film was scanned and given to the Weta Digital camera department. The dimensions and perspective of the mountainside were matched and duplicated in a wire-frame grid in a computer modelling programme – Maya – and the extra landscaping modelled into that, along with the archway, steps and bridge. Textures were taken from the filmed rocks, and painted onto the digital ones to tie the whole thing together. It works, partly because of the skills of the modellers and compositors, but mainly because we are so misty eyed over the loss of Gandalf that we can barely see the rocks, let alone look for where they are joined.

While we were on the mountainside clouds moved in, and the helicopters had to desert us for a while. But it was a beautiful place to be stranded, and a welcome lacuna in our hectic schedule.

LOTHLÓRIEN

I don't think I've ever seen any pictures which come close to matching the evocative strength of Tolkien's writing about Lothlórien, including my own. It is not a matter of simply translating his descriptions into pictorial form, because their strength is not so much in the pictures they conjure up, as in the feelings they evoke, and I think these feelings are derived from something quite primordial – a connection with the forest that was broken in the early years of mankind's development; a lost paradise that part of us still yearns for.

This comes through in all of Tolkien's writings about nature, but it seems to take on an extra power in those episodes concerning trees and forests, and Lothlórien in particular becomes not just the heart of the remaining Elven kingdoms, but almost the soul of Middle-earth itself.

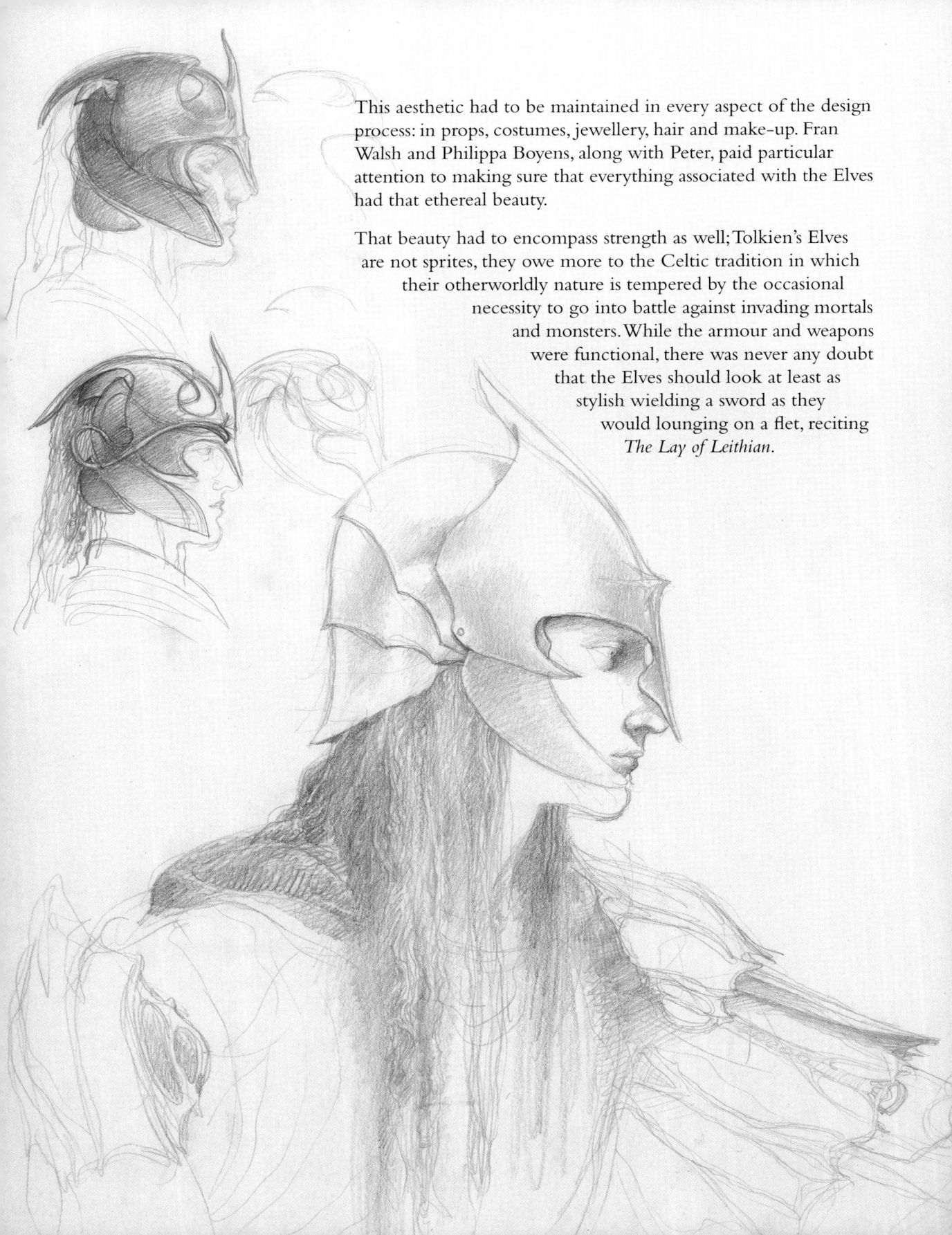

This aesthetic had to be maintained in every aspect of the design process: in props, costumes, jewellery, hair and make-up. Fran Walsh and Philippa Boyens, along with Peter, paid particular attention to making sure that everything associated with the Elves had that ethereal beauty.

That beauty had to encompass strength as well; Tolkien's Elves are not sprites, they owe more to the Celtic tradition in which their otherworldly nature is tempered by the occasional necessity to go into battle against invading mortals and monsters. While the armour and weapons were functional, there was never any doubt that the Elves should look at least as stylish wielding a sword as they would lounging on a flet, reciting *The Lay of Leithian*.

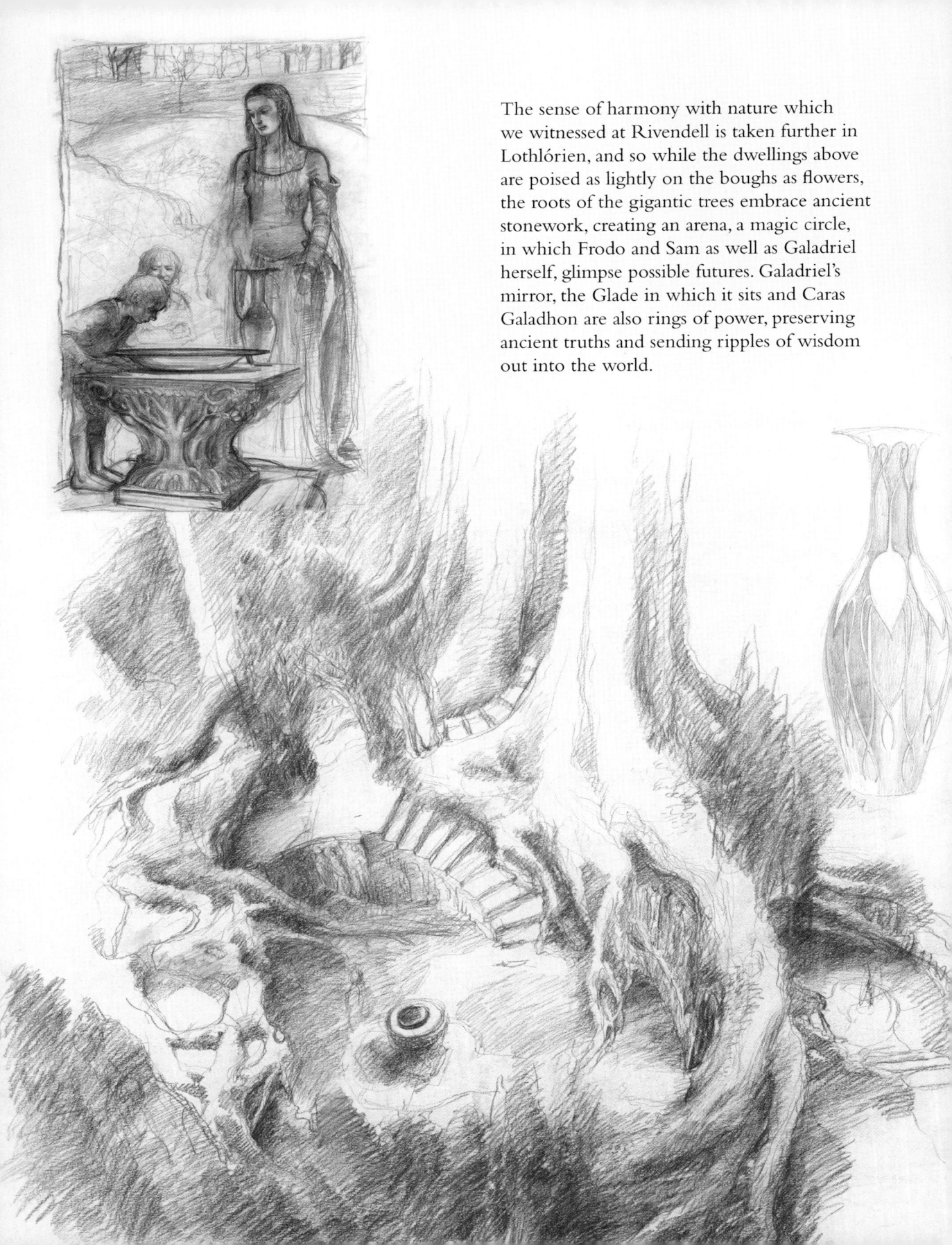

The sense of harmony with nature which we witnessed at Rivendell is taken further in Lothlórien, and so while the dwellings above are poised as lightly on the boughs as flowers, the roots of the gigantic trees embrace ancient stonework, creating an arena, a magic circle, in which Frodo and Sam as well as Galadriel herself, glimpse possible futures. Galadriel's mirror, the Glade in which it sits and Caras Galadhon are also rings of power, preserving ancient truths and sending ripples of wisdom out into the world.

Galadriel is an archetypal figure; one of a long line of fays and faerie queens that run through our literary heritage, offering guidance, reproach or a shining ideal to generations of brave – but hesitant or forgetful – questing heroes. As a seer her pedigree goes back to the Sybils of the ancient world; as an immortal to the earliest images of the Earth-mother, and as a giver of magical gifts she is the fairy god-mother of countless tales. She is also the fairy helper, who will appear at crucial moments and offer advice, a charm or a simple item which will turn out to be a light to ward off monsters, a rope to scale a cliff, or a cloak to conceal you from your enemies.

BORDERLANDS

The monumental figures which mark the most northerly extent of the ancient kingdom of Gondor, the Argonath, are carved from the cliffs that rear above the Anduin. We thought that the topmost parts of the statues could be added on in the form of courses of stone-work, quarried from either side. A beautiful miniature was created at Weta, which included a substantial part of the gorge, and this was blended into the shots filmed on location.

Throughout the films use is made of an enormous amount of artificial stone moulded from rocks and the cliffs around Wellington's coastline. It seems to work at any scale, whether dotted with tiny miniature trees, or framing a close-up of a hobbit's foot.

It was at this point that we needed to make decisions about the design of the crowns of the old kings, because these would need to be reflected in the look of the ancient armour, the many statues and architectural features in Minas Tirith and the crown which will be used at Aragorn's coronation.

More ancient ruins are to be found at Amon Hen. Although the text makes reference to the Seat of Seeing itself and the area immediately around it, and the old, cracked steps leading there, we thought that there might be an excuse to create some more extensive ruins. As a site of some significance, the remains of other structures would have accumulated around it and there may be evidence of this. When we were looking at the location for the first time I did a small drawing in the pocket-sized sketchbook that I always carry with me, of Boromir and the corpses of his assailants beneath the dead gaze of a monumental head, lying on its side with a fallen tree leaning against it. I thought that it could make an appropriate background for those dramatic and moving moments, and might even feature in some stuntwork – fight directors are always on the lookout for objects that people can fall off – but Peter had an even better use for it, as the sad and silent witness of Boromir's surrender to temptation and his attempt to wrest the Ring from Frodo.

Speaking of stuntwork, the Seeing Seat was the scene of a fall from grace for me too. I had followed Sam Genet, the sculptor – one of the unsung heroes of the whole enterprise, by the way, carving acres of stonework, cliff faces and architectural features across the length and breadth of our Middle-earth – to look at a detail in his carving of the Seat when part of the polystyrene collapsed beneath me and I fell, breaking my wrist. The first question on everyone's lips was ' . . . which hand?', but I was back at my desk within a couple of hours, my left arm in plaster, and the right scribbling away, making up for lost time.

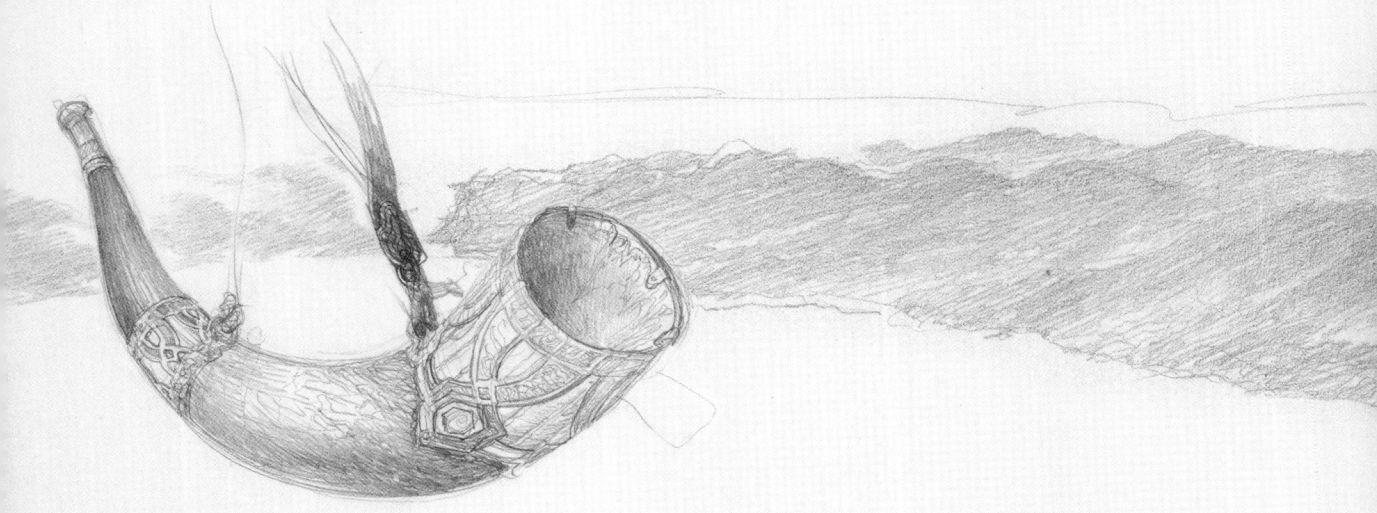

Throughout the filming and the period leading up to it, we had been so involved in the tasks immediately facing us that it was not at all easy to judge how *The Fellowship of the Ring* might turn out. We knew that we had an excellent cast, script and director, and that we had all worked to the maximum of our capabilities, but also that there are times when all the right ingredients appear to be in place, and the magic just fails to happen. To everyone's relief and pleasure, Peter emerged from the cutting room with something that was beyond our expectations, a film that was as moving and profound as it was spectacular and dramatic, and which redefined what a 'fantasy' film could do. The music and sound, the effects, and the sets that we had laboured over for so long were now in their rightful place, supporting a compelling story. It was seeing the characters brought so vividly to life, though, that gave me the greatest pleasure.

I've tried to think of a film that could be seen as a precursor, a model that had to be matched, but there isn't one really. What there is, for me, is a memory of the impression made by certain films seen in childhood, or books, or genres encountered for the first time; the visceral excitement felt when a new story – a new world – is being opened up, and you know that you are in the hands of a master storyteller.

ROHAN

We seem to enter a larger, and perhaps more grown-up world when we find ourselves following the trail of the captive hobbits across the wide expanses of the plains of Rohan. Creatures of Myth and Legend still inhabit the forests and craggy mountainsides, but we are now in a land dominated by a vigorous warrior people, the Rohirrim, and a world in which human tragedy and the effects of those long-rumoured wars are more in evidence.

The job of creating arms and armour for the riders and a breed of opponents worthy of them was taken up enthusiastically by Richard's designers at Weta. Getting a formidable and iconic look for the Uruk-hai was the end result of a long period of development and design in which my more 'storybook' efforts were soon overtaken.

FANGORN

I love drawing trees and forests. It is like drawing people with an endless capacity to stretch and twist, their history recorded in every scar and irregularity – and they will hold their pose for years! Invented woodlands, hopefully informed by long hours spent sketching in real ones, give an opportunity to draw and design with freedom as well as delicacy, as long as you remember that trees have an anatomy as well.

The competing forces that affect the growth of a tree – gravity, the wind and the need for light – can be read in the contortions of branches and the form of the trunk. Like skin, the bark only partially conceals the structure underneath, and in old trees is frequently rotted or broken away. Drawing trees is more an act of empathy than analysis, though, and I seem to find it a little easier now than I did when I was a sapling.

In pre-Christian times and pagan societies there was a widespread belief that trees contained spirits which could inflict punishment on those who attacked them without making the proper observances, and the Ents and Huorns of Fangorn forest are a perfect embodiment of that idea. Treebeard as a character is a wonderfully original creation, but his antecedents are as old as the hills. The epic of *Gilgamesh* tells of a battle between the hero (from the city of Uruk) and Humbaba, the guardian of the cedar forests. Humbaba is slain, to the dismay of the gods, and the cedars destroyed, just as the sacred groves of northern Europe were destroyed by zealous crusaders. But forests still have the ability to inspire us with awe and reverence, and the feeling that we are amongst sentient beings, and Tolkien's work is a poetic and moving reminder of that.

EDORAS

When Tolkien described Meduseld, I'm sure that he was also thinking of Heorot, the 'horn-gabled' feast-hall of Hrothgar, King of the Geats, in the Anglo-Saxon poem *Beowulf*. I had done a painting of this for an earlier book, *Castles*, and that became a starting point for designs for the Golden Hall. It is wooden, but I wanted it to be decorated and strengthened by lots of gold and ironwork, and assumed that the importance of the horse in Rohan culture would be reflected in the details of the building.

We found the perfect location for Edoras in a valley in the South Island. I think it was as close to Tolkien's description as it was possible to get, and we built the hall, the stables and the main gate, with a few other buildings around them, on a craggy outcrop surrounded by magnificent mountains. For wider shots we needed the rest of the city, and the extra buildings were modelled digitally and painted and lit to match the real ones.

In the ornate and aged splendour of the Golden Hall, a timeless drama is played out as the forces of decay and corruption are banished and the king restored to health. In Théoden's recovery there are echoes of the grail-quest story of the Fisher King, whose wound can only be healed by the right words, the questions of a seeker after truth. With the healing of the king the wasteland that he presides over is made fertile again, and the citizens given new hope.

The confrontation between Gandalf and Saruman's agent, Gríma Wormtongue, carries strong resonances too: the manipulative counsellor, exerting power from behind the throne, and the struggle between honesty and deceit for the soul of a nation are part of a pattern we all recognise ... or perhaps it is just that I'm writing this in the middle of a general election campaign.

As with the Anglo-Saxons, Rohan legends contain references to dragons, great boars and other extraordinary beasts, and these were used extensively in the many decorative features of Meduseld and the surrounding buildings. The horse is prominent of course – especially in the stables – but there are many other more fantastic creatures winding around the pillars and doorways, and over the fine metalwork, turning the building itself into a record of an ancient and rich culture.

The figures of Théoden's ancestor Eorl riding Felaróf, from whom Shadowfax is descended, are woven into a tapestry which features prominently in Tolkien's description of the Golden Hall. We made eight others, some illustrating events recounted in the appendices of *The Lord of the Rings* such as the slaying of the dragon, Scatha, and the story of the death of Eorl's father as he attempted to tame the wild horse, and some referring to characters and tales too obscure to be recorded. I was quite happy with the finished results of them all, except for the main one, and though I worked through the night trying to salvage it for use on set the next day, it didn't match the splendour of the rest of the Golden Hall, or Tolkien's evocative description. Not knowing how much of any of the tapestries would be seen, but fearing that the camera may just settle on that one, it was left to languish in the props store.

HELM'S DEEP

I started working on designs for Helm's Deep on my first day in New Zealand, in January 1998. Peter knew that it was going to play an important part in the film, and he wanted to be able to start planning the battle and the build-up to it. I carry strong memories of time spent as a child, building fortresses out of cardboard, and making sandcastles on the beach – with epic narratives running through my head – and soon realised that Peter's intense interest in the miniatures had a similar basis; we were creating arenas in which we could amaze ourselves.

Within a couple of weeks, working with Grant and Richard, we had sorted out the design, and work on a maquette for the miniature was begun. We worked in clay to model the valley because it is such a quick and malleable material, even though it is doomed to fall apart soon after you push it into a corner and forget about it – but we were able to have the maquette scanned and get the larger 1/35th scale miniature started before it followed the sandcastles into oblivion.

Drawing figures in action have some inherent difficulties: models can't be expected to hold dramatic poses for any length of time without looking awkward or bored, and photographs of people in action – even when copied closely – invariably look wrong. Placing them in a crowded and confused battle scene makes it easier; when one figure starts to look unconvincing, you can position another in front of the offending knee, or whatever part of the drawing is giving you problems, and shields can be as useful to an erring artist as to a knight errant. As the scenes get larger it becomes impractical to do anything other than draw from the imagination, and the extra distance is very forgiving.

A drawing like the one opposite, done without any preparatory work, and without reference to models or photographs, can hold up pretty well until you start to turn it into a painting. All the small flaws in the drawing are suddenly exposed by taking it a step closer to a representation of reality, and what might have looked charming in the drawing starts to look inept. After taking a drawing to this stage I'll refine it as much as I can, usually on tracing paper, and do further studies of individual figures. This can easily result in characters in a painting losing some of their vitality, and I'll end up with perfectly proportioned figures that look a little wooden. Sometimes I feel that my trees have more life in them than my people.

The attack by Treebeard and his army of Ents and Huorns on Isengard was one of the more difficult effects sequences tackled during post-production on *The Two Towers*. One issue was the question of how to convey the idea of the Ents diverting the river so that it floods Isengard, in a simple and exciting manner. A montage of shots showing Ents involved in various forms of civil engineering would be an awkward thing to manage, and so having them destroy a conveniently sited dam seemed an elegant and visually satisfying solution.

*The cold hard lands
they bites our hands,
they gnaws our feet.
The rocks and stones
are like old bones
all bare of meat.*

THE ROAD TO MORDOR

Gollum is, almost literally, a shadow archetype, the part of ourselves that we most fear and deny; a creature that has crawled out from the depths of our psyche and follows in our footsteps, as a constant reminder of what we may become. The challenge of working such complexity into an animated, computer-generated character was taken on with relish by Andy Serkis, and everyone else involved in his creation.

*Alive without breath;
as cold as death;
never thirsting, ever drinking;
clad in mail, never clinking.*

Marshlands, bogs and fens feature strongly in our heritage of legends and folklore because large tracts of Europe were once covered by them and, like the forests, they were a refuge for outlaws and those living on the borders of society. They formed natural defences where a small group of rebels with local knowledge could defy and confound a larger pursuing force. They were also places of sacrifice, and some of the well-preserved victims have been yielded up as eloquent though silent witnesses to the times in which they lived, and their own tragic ends.

Sméagol led Frodo and Sam to a vantage point and hiding place overlooking the Black Gate – the entrance to Mordor – and rested there for a while, patiently, while I tried to decide what the Towers of the Teeth should look like. John arrived at his excellent designs for the miniature used in the film a little more directly – with more than just a couple of weary hobbits waiting for him – and I provided the mechanism which is used to open the gate, and a new role and change of clothes for the cave-troll from Moria.

I decided that this would make a good cover image for the centenary edition while working on the painting. It shows some of the major protagonists at a crucial point in the story, and is immediately recognisable. The fact that the book and its author are so well known meant that there was little need to create a louder image, and the typography could also be fairly restrained.

ITHILIEN

Grey as a mouse,
Big as a house,
Nose like a snake,
I make the earth shake,
As I tramp through the grass;
Trees crack as I pass.

Sam's verse is not quite a riddle, since he reveals that its subject is an 'Oliphaunt', but it owes much to the tradition of riddle-making that is preserved in folklore and manuscripts such as the Old English *Exeter Book*. Tolkien obviously loved this material, and uses it as a plot device, as well as for its value as entertainment; these playful exercises in metaphor can have profound consequences, as Bilbo discovers when challenged to a riddle-contest by Gollum. I suspect that, given the value placed on the bardic tradition in earlier times, they may have had some ritual significance, as well as providing a training ground for the composers of epic poetry. Anyway, here's one of mine –

Dug up from the earth and sealed in a coffin,
sold for less than my true worth,
hacked by sharp blades, and dragged over a wide meadow
behind a pale charioteer,
leaving, I hope, some evidence of the crime.

Now shrunken in size
having lived my life backwards,
my slow demise
another's conception.
What am I?

Every time I work through the night to meet a deadline, I swear that it will be the last time. It is usually completely counter-productive, and I'll find myself struggling foggily through the next day trying to rectify mistakes to an illustration made at four o'clock in the morning, when a good night's sleep would have been more helpful. I found that as the pace of production on the film became more hectic, this syndrome – which I'd hoped I'd left behind in England – started to reappear, and there were many nights when Grant Major and I would keep company with the night shift, trying to get a set ready for the crew's arrival at 6am.

The forbidden pool was one of those tricky sets which couldn't be pre-fabricated, and had to be built in situ in a great hurry. The fact that it contained a waterfall, which it shared with the set of Faramir's cave, and was crammed into one of the smaller studios, compounded the difficulties. I thought that we had made elegant and economical use of the space, and it would have been perfect if it hadn't also had to accommodate the actors, the film crew and all their equipment. It was a little embarrassing, but quite funny, to go back later in the day and see them perched on every available rock, like the pixies in Santa's grotto.

Exterior sets were usually a more enjoyable experience for everyone. The sites would have been chosen for some interesting quality that Peter wanted to capture; with the cross-roads scene it was the ruined look of some of the trees, as though armies had been marching through the woods. Our headless king statue was lowered into place – with a little difficulty, and the crude Orkish addition fixed on top. We wanted to leave other evidence of their presence and so, while broken branches were strewn on the ground, we painted Orc graffiti around the base of the statue. We didn't really know what the Orcs would have to say, or what their scribblings would look like; I produced a selection of idle scrawls and foul symbols myself, and then left the painters to it.

Minas Morgul, the diseased and corrupted sister-city to Minas Tirith, glowing with its eerie corpse-light and reeking with foul vapours, is one of the great haunted castles of world literature; a fascinating and horrible creation, and an impressive introduction to the succession of terrifying experiences that lie in wait for our heroes as they enter Mordor.

All of the fortifications that surround Mordor were built by the Númenóreans in order to contain Sauron, but as his power returned they were taken and occupied by his forces and given an Orkish makeover; the ruinous stonework crowned with rusty iron spikes and crude hovels erected in courtyards. I designed a small set for a brief glimpse of the Witch-king preparing for war, but it would have been interesting to have seen a little more of what lies behind those glowing walls. With its noxious fumes and malevolent Ringwraiths, Minas Morgul couldn't have been the most desirable posting for an Orc foot-soldier.

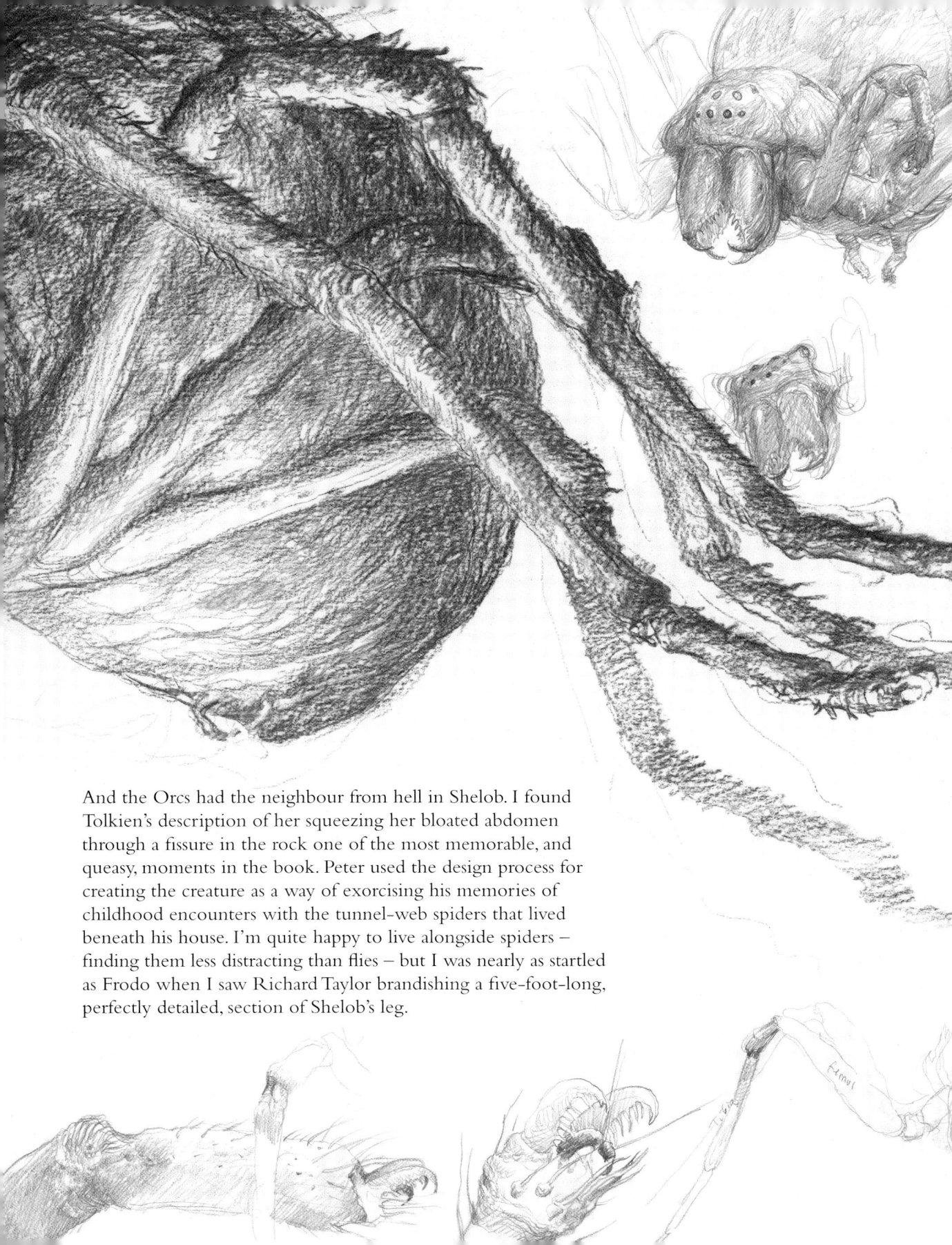

And the Orcs had the neighbour from hell in Shelob. I found Tolkien's description of her squeezing her bloated abdomen through a fissure in the rock one of the most memorable, and queasy, moments in the book. Peter used the design process for creating the creature as a way of exorcising his memories of childhood encounters with the tunnel-web spiders that lived beneath his house. I'm quite happy to live alongside spiders – finding them less distracting than flies – but I was nearly as startled as Frodo when I saw Richard Taylor brandishing a five-foot-long, perfectly detailed, section of Shelob's leg.

The Orcs stationed at Cirith Ungol, Gorbag and Shagrat and their quarrelsome troops, give a small insight into the way of life of some of Sauron's minions, and it looks pretty bleak and unrewarding. I've often thought that the story of the War of the Ring, told from the point of view of an Orc foot-soldier, would offer an interesting new perspective.

Orcs and the Uruk-hai were, arguably, bred by Melkor and Sauron from captured Elves, transformed by torture and sorcery, but I'm not sure if they could breed amongst themselves. Tolkien uses the phrase 'maggot brood', possibly refering to the Norse creation myth of Ymir, the giant whose flesh and bones formed the Earth and its rocky mountains while the trolls and dark elves, and other subterranean creatures, were hatched within his corpse. It's a poor start in life, but they must have some redeeming features – a sentimental attachment to glittering objects, perhaps, or the occasional twinge of self-pity.

MINAS TIRITH

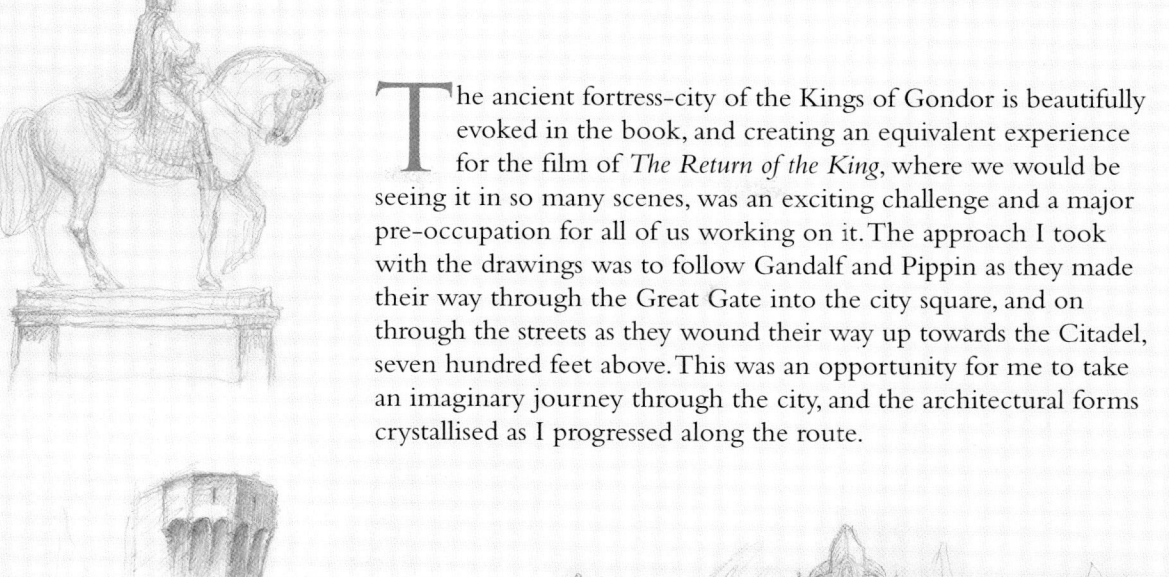

The ancient fortress-city of the Kings of Gondor is beautifully evoked in the book, and creating an equivalent experience for the film of *The Return of the King*, where we would be seeing it in so many scenes, was an exciting challenge and a major pre-occupation for all of us working on it. The approach I took with the drawings was to follow Gandalf and Pippin as they made their way through the Great Gate into the city square, and on through the streets as they wound their way up towards the Citadel, seven hundred feet above. This was an opportunity for me to take an imaginary journey through the city, and the architectural forms crystallised as I progressed along the route.

Alongside the drawings, I worked on a Plasticine maquette, so that Peter could see and make comments on the overall shape as it evolved. Then we moved on to a larger maquette, with modelmakers John Baster and Mary MacLachlan taking on the bulk of the work, and a larger team working on the final miniature. There were so many buildings in this and the Osgiliath miniature that we pre-fabricated a large number of architectural elements – pillars, arches, windows and walls – as a kit-set so that each of the modelmakers could produce a variety of buildings, serving different purposes, while maintaining a cohesive style.

All the major buildings – the gates, citadel, Houses of Healing, the garrison, and anything that we would need to reproduce as a set – were carefully designed, and some were also made at a larger scale so that they would bear closer scrutiny, but the $1/72$nd scale miniature of the whole city was so beautifully finished that the camera was able to get closer to it than anyone had imagined.

The Art Department built a large Minas Tirith set, incorporating the first and second gates, a network of streets and alleys and a section of wall. The drawings on this page were made for a small set that was built during post-production on *The Return of the King* for some extra scenes such as that between Gandalf and Pippin as they prepare for the worst as trolls are battering at the gates. Our aim with these sets was to give Peter and Andrew Lesnie as many choices as possible, and to recreate the kind of feeling you get when walking through an old Italian city for the first time, with intriguing alleyways, steps and archways leading off in different directions.

We created a lot of decorative stone carving, fountains and courtyards, and paid particular attention to the statues that were to be seen in many of the streets, and the effigies of the Kings of Gondor that stand on either side of Denethor's hall. Our team of sculptors; Brigitte Wuest, Heather Kilgour, Natalie Staniforth, Kirk Nicholls, Paul Dean, Gary Hunt, Nathan Hall and Virginia Lee, as well as the tireless and talented team of Sam Genet and Ra Vincent, produced a great deal of excellent work. At times the workshop resembled something that might have been seen in Renaissance Italy, if it weren't for the chunks of polystyrene flying in all directions, whipped up into a snowstorm by that relentless Wellington wind.

The throne room, where Denethor sits forlornly holding the pieces of Boromir's broken horn, was the last set completed during our marathon shoot. It shared space in a warehouse on Wellington's waterfront with the edge of Fangorn forest. Kathryn Lim, the lead painter on that set, did much to create a timeless classical quality, with walls, pillars and floors all finished as cool, beautiful marble. This was also my last all-night session – spent giving the statues a little more patina, and aloft in a cherry-picker applying a gold mosaic finish to the ceilings in the aisles – something that impressed itself into my memory, if not into celluloid. I did finally get my mosaic ceiling, though – three years later when designing the CG set extension for the wide shots – and Photoshop was a much easier way of doing it.

When illustrating the centenary edition, there was a technical constraint in that the art paper that the illustrations were to be printed on could only be bound around sections of text paper. Since I wanted every illustration to be directly related to the text on the opposite page – I find it irritating to turn to a picture that relates to something I read about five pages previously – I let this arbitrary factor dictate which scenes I was going to illustrate. This made it easier for me in some ways; I wouldn't need to spend time deciding which were the fifty best moments in the book, and the text is so rich, with interesting things happening on every page, that I would not be at a loss for what to draw.

It can be slightly frustrating though, to miss hitting a point in the text that you would love to illustrate; the prince of Dol Amroth is a character that I've only painted once before – on a little wooden panel that hung in Pippin's room in Minas Tirith – and he arrives on the scene, accompanied by mounted knights and gilded banners, just a couple of pages beyond the one that the picture opposite was designed for – not far behind Forlong the Fat, Lord of Lossarnach, who I don't think anyone has ever drawn.

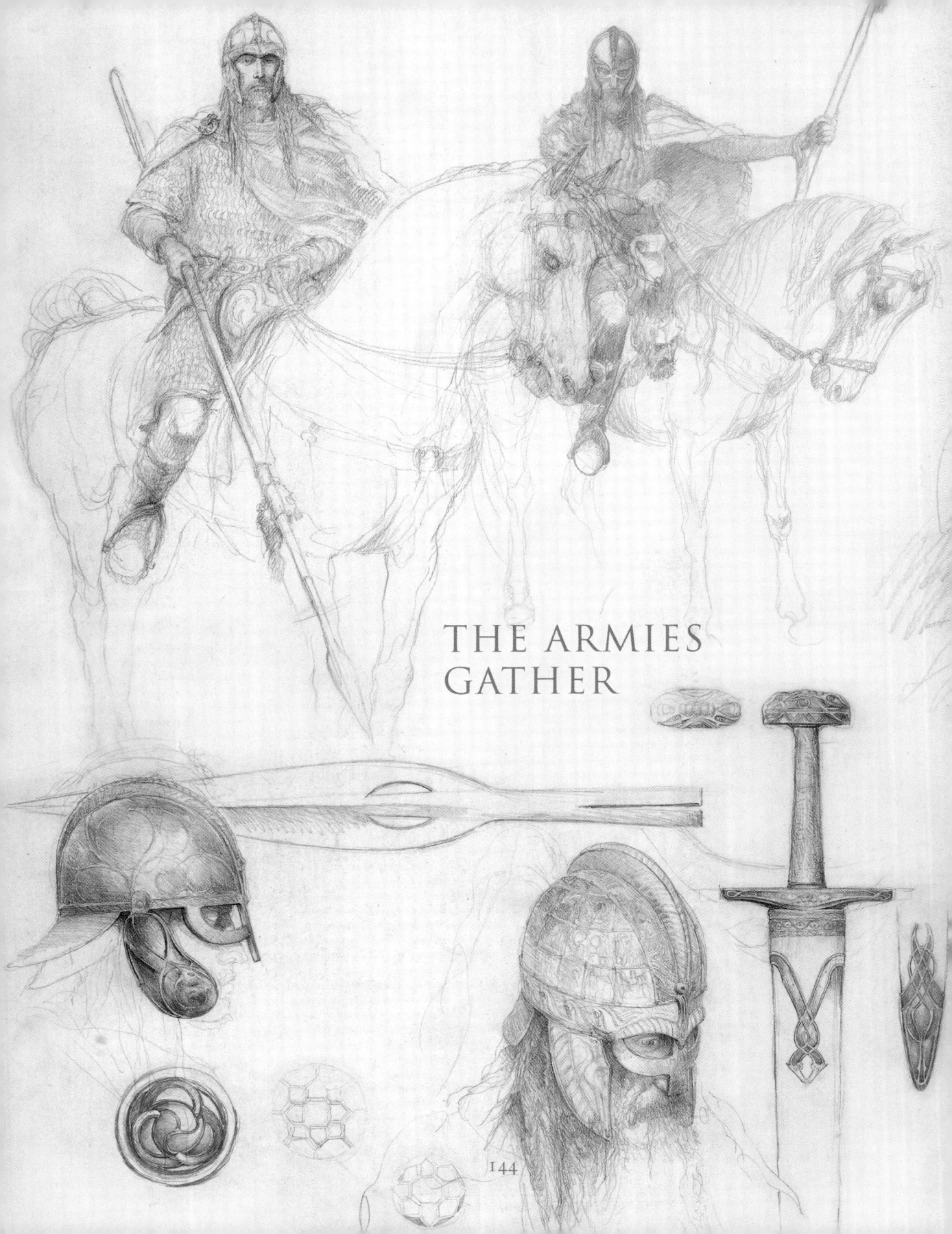

THE ARMIES GATHER

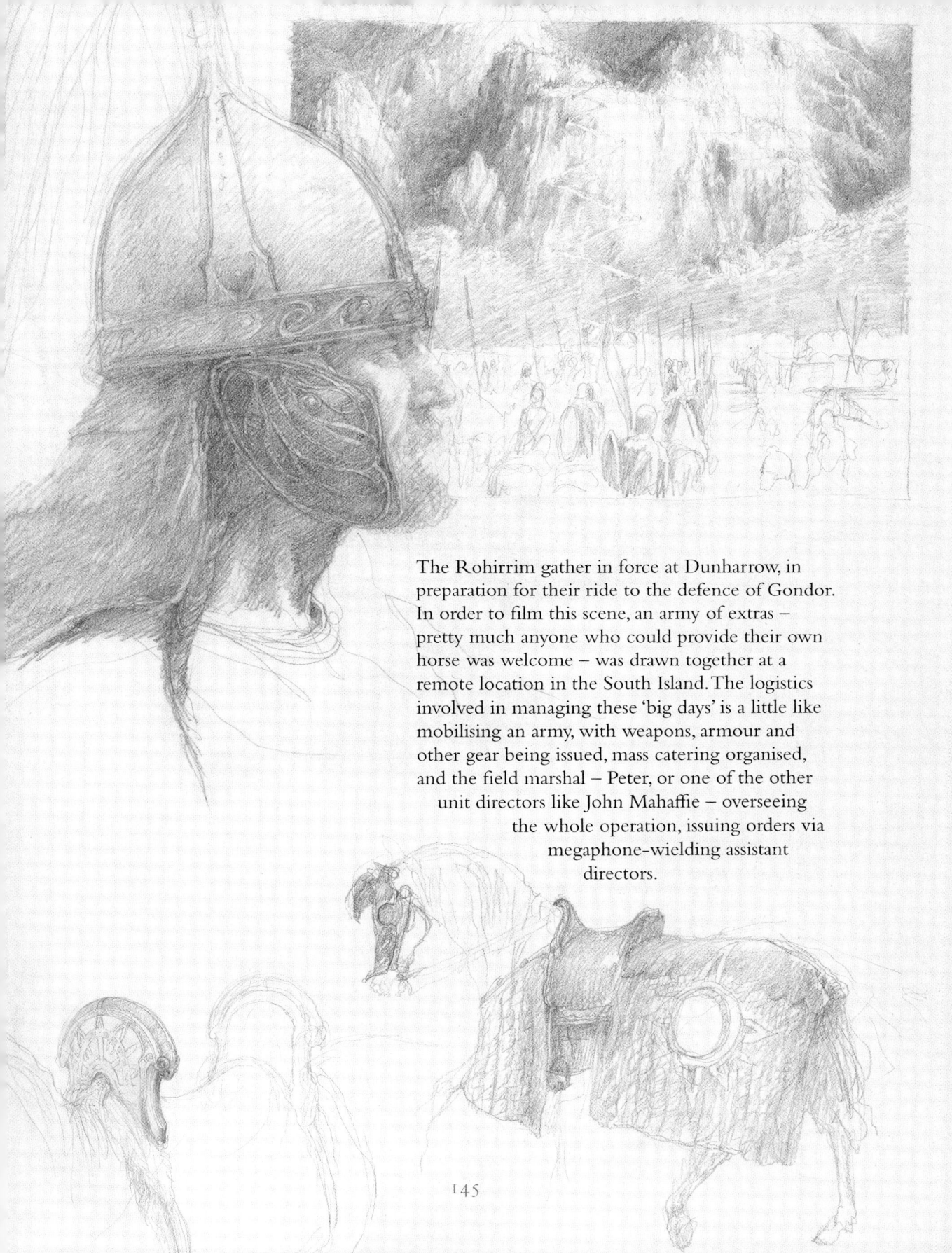

The Rohirrim gather in force at Dunharrow, in preparation for their ride to the defence of Gondor. In order to film this scene, an army of extras — pretty much anyone who could provide their own horse was welcome — was drawn together at a remote location in the South Island. The logistics involved in managing these 'big days' is a little like mobilising an army, with weapons, armour and other gear being issued, mass catering organised, and the field marshal — Peter, or one of the other unit directors like John Mahaffie — overseeing the whole operation, issuing orders via megaphone-wielding assistant directors.

The troops on the ground would later be supplemented by a vast digital reserve, ranked according to their degree of detail, from heroes in the foreground to those with the lowest resolution in the far distance. A wide shot like the one below, filmed on a small set in Wellington in front of a bluescreen and some trucks, would be extended with a miniature and a photographic background shot from a helicopter in a remote part of the southern alps. Digital tents, campfires, horses and riders were added once everything else was in place.

An army of the dead was summoned up from the depths of Weta Digital. I did a little bit of work on their look, as well as designing backgrounds and miniatures for the shots. At this stage I was working in the Visual Effects Art Department with Jeremy Bennett and Gus Hunter. We were producing artwork – mainly in Photoshop – for the effects shots being handed over by Peter as he was cutting the film. Every few days we would gather in his cutting room as he talked through the new material, then we would collect frames as jpegs from Editorial and set to work.

Complex compositions – with a lot of figures – can be quite difficult to organise if you feel that you need a highly resolved drawing before starting to work in watercolour. I made several, increasingly confused, attempts with this illustration before launching into it, painting the Orc at the very bottom first, and then the one behind him, working my way back into the melee and up the blank page with nothing other than a very rough drawing as a guide. When I got about halfway up I put a piece of tracing paper over the top and drew the rest of the figures more carefully, and with a clearer idea of what I was doing.

THE BLOW FALLS

The Battle of the Pelennor Fields, while not quite the climax of the story, represents a turning point, the moment when Sauron's forces, and his will, are successfully resisted. The Witch-king, his lieutenant, launches the attack from Minas Morgul and quickly over-runs Osgiliath, the ruined city that lies at the centre of the disputed territory.

THE STEWARD'S TOMB

My memories of working in a cemetery, reading Edgar Allan Poe and wandering in a Pre-Raphaelite daze through the atmospheric necropolis in Highgate, were finally put to some use when designing the Hallows – where the Kings and Stewards of Gondor were laid to rest. This only exists as a miniature, but we made a beautiful marble interior, with effigies and other sculptural details, as a setting for Denethor's dramatic and fiery exit.

Grond

When Grond is pulled across the battlefield by trolls and 'great beasts' and swung against the huge and heavily decorated gates of Minas Tirith, its fiery, brutal jaws are also tearing into the bronze figures of the city's historical defenders and leaders. Each blow is an attempt to obliterate the Gondorian culture, as well as gain access to its last redoubt.

Grond was designed and built at Weta as a miniature, though at even a quarter of its full-scale size, it was an awe-inspiring sight, and looked capable of doing a great deal of damage.

Grond is named after the mace that Morgoth used in his wars against the Noldor; known as the 'Hammer of the Underworld', it left great, gaping wounds in the earth, and sounded like thunder. It is forged in the image of a huge, ravening wolf, and this evokes memories of Carcharoth, the wolf that guarded Morgoth's fortress, as well as Fenrir, who would be unleashed during Ragnarok, the final battle between the gods and giants of Norse mythology.

Stories of cataclysmic battles in which supernatural or monstrous creatures are ranged against each other, alongside human combatants, occur in most cultures and in epic literature, from the Celtic *Battle of the Trees* to the *Maharabhata*. They invoke the interplay of primal forces and natural calamity, but are probably also mythologised memories of wars and skirmishes between different tribes or societies, in which a new weapon, or the potent deity invoked by their opponents, makes a lasting impression on those most bruised by the encounter.

Whenever there is an opportunity locally to observe horses doing anything other than cropping grass, I will be close by with a camera or sketchbook, continuing a lifelong quest to understand and absorb all their shifting forms and finely tuned mechanics. I have no shortage of reference books, but simply copying a photograph just doesn't work for me. I've studiously copied George Stubbs' anatomical engravings, and pored over photographs by Eadweard Muybridge of horses in motion, but accept that I'll always have to draw several badly before drawing one well.

Other beasts can also be challenging: the smell of a fell beast is something that is hard to capture in a drawing, although that is the thing that the author evokes most clearly. Every real animal, from a dinosaur to a dormouse, has an anatomical structure that follows a basic pattern – where there are deviations it is usually possible to see how they occurred – and this formula can also be stretched into the shape of any creature we may wish to imagine.

CIRITH UNGOL

Creatures of stone, animated by malice, guard the gates of Cirith Ungol. The Watchers create an invisible barrier, and utter a dreadful shriek to raise the alarm. Tolkien had described the figures quite clearly and, as in much of the design work for the films, we were trying to create that sense of immediate recognition, so that we, and the audience, know exactly where we are, and that these places are more than an imaginary construct. If people can say 'that is exactly the way I saw it too', then that shared vision starts to become more concrete.

Often there is only a few hours – or even minutes – between a set being finished and dressed and setting up for the first shot, and that can provide a brief opportunity to enjoy it as a complete environment. It is when they are lit, though, that the sets are at their most beautiful, and then it becomes the realm of the actors and film crew. If I am there, watching from the shadows, it is usually because we are waiting for an opportunity to show Peter some new drawings; otherwise we are too busy trying to meet our deadline for the next polystyrene and plaster edifice.

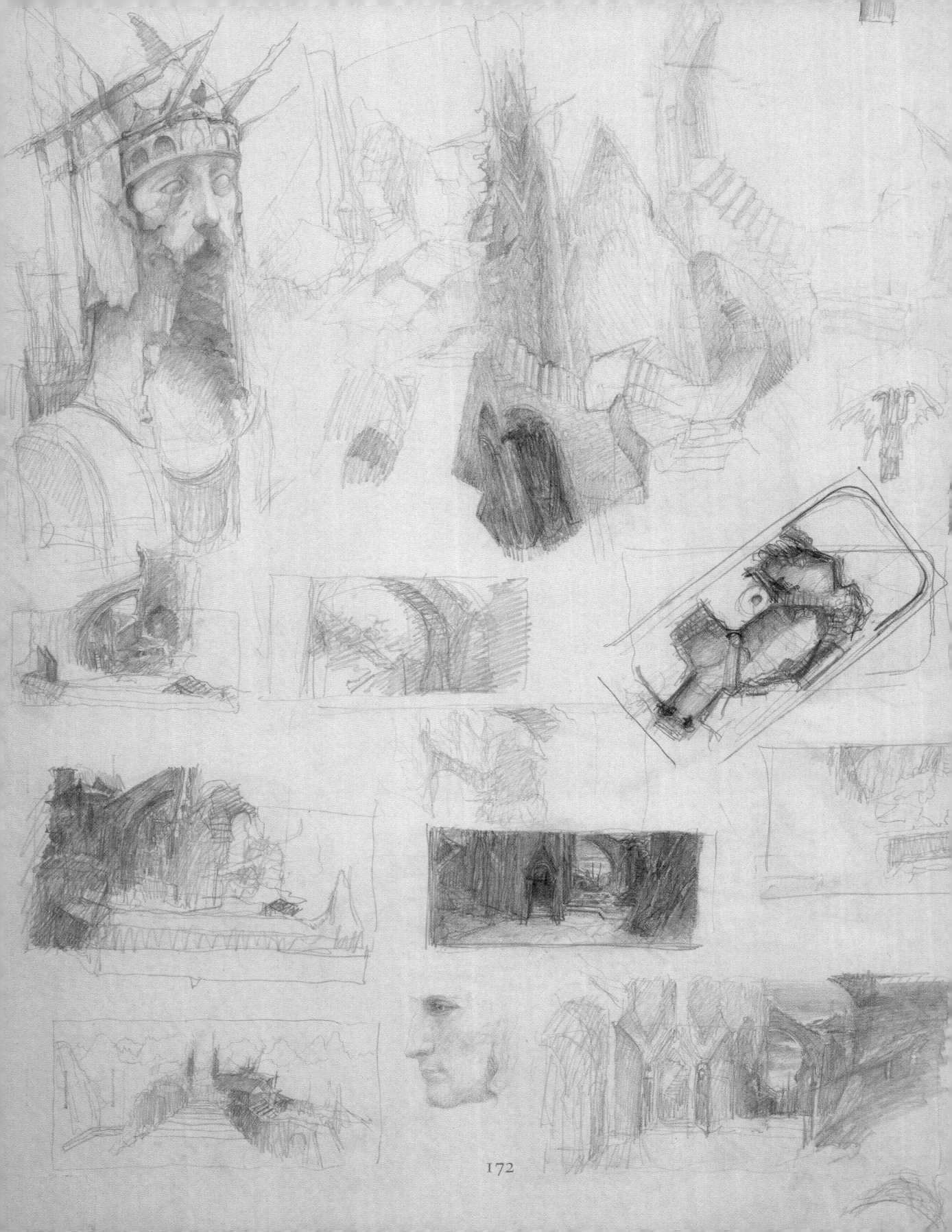

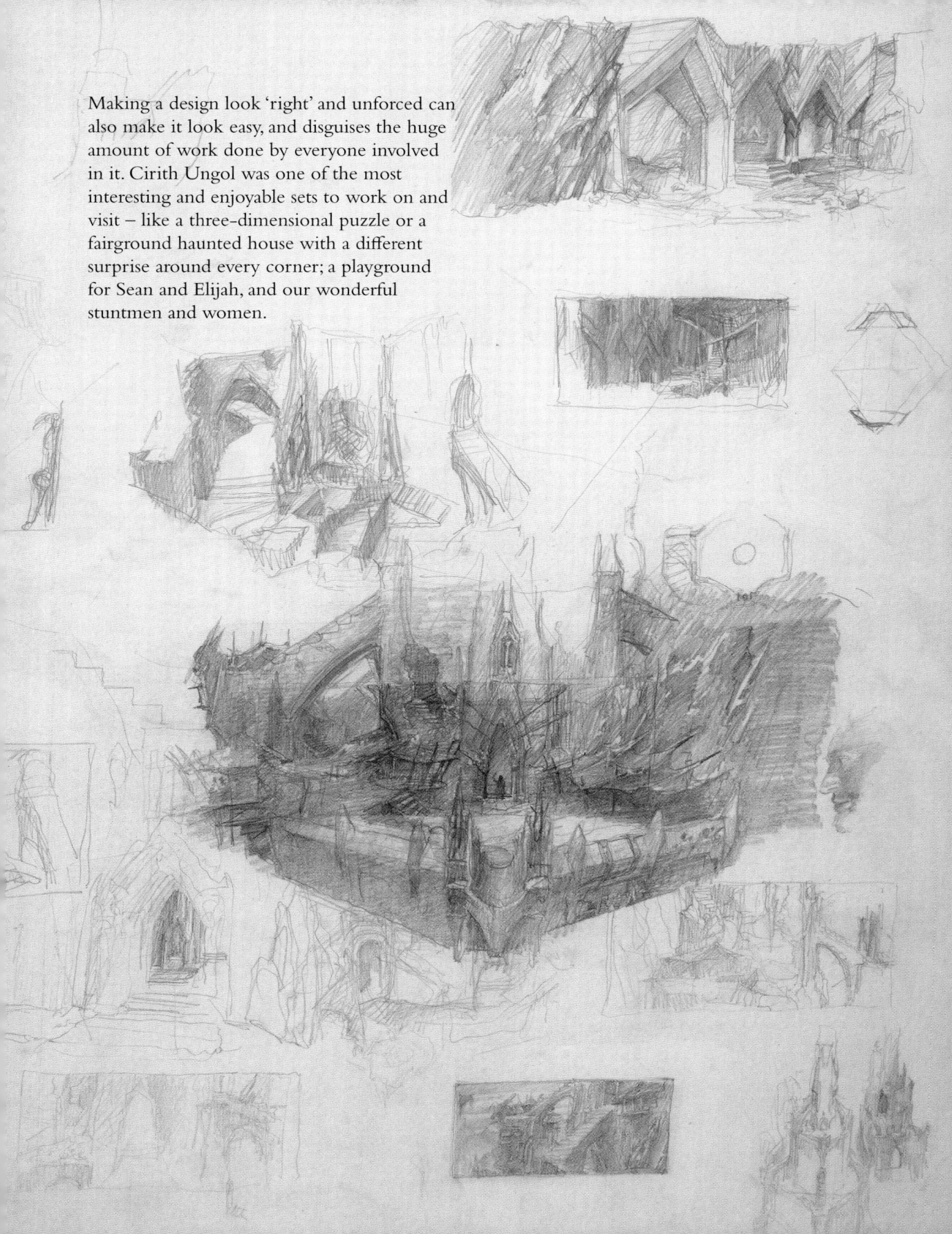

Making a design look 'right' and unforced can also make it look easy, and disguises the huge amount of work done by everyone involved in it. Cirith Ungol was one of the most interesting and enjoyable sets to work on and visit – like a three-dimensional puzzle or a fairground haunted house with a different surprise around every corner; a playground for Sean and Elijah, and our wonderful stuntmen and women.

This isn't an Orkish firing squad; it's just my attempts to sort out the drawing of one little archer while his more composed big friend on the right looks on. It's also a demonstration of the effects on an ill-disciplined mind of spending too much time in the company of Orcs.

MORDOR

Though here at journey's end I lie
in darkness buried deep,
beyond all towers strong and high,
beyond all mountains steep,
above all shadows rides the Sun
and Stars for ever dwell:
I will not say the Day is done,
nor bid the Stars farewell.

Orodruin poured forth rivers of molten rock from chasms in its sides. Some would flow blazing towards Barad-Dur down great channels — some would wend their way into the stony plain until they cooled and lay like twisted dragon shapes vomited from the tormented earth.

The fiery glow glared against the stark rock faces so that they seemed to be drenched with blood.

Gollum and the Ring in the Crack of Doom, and Barad-dûr fallen and the forces of Sauron in disarray and ruin; it was time to start thinking about going home. I had been working in New Zealand for just over six years on the trilogy and the extended edition DVDs. It had been an exhilarating, though at times exhausting, life-changing experience, but I needed to be back in my own studio and watching spring unfold in my own Shire.

When you are working on something that intensively, for that length of time, events outside of your everyday concerns seem strangely accelerated and remote, like a film running at high speed. Wars are fought, governments fall, people meet, marry and have two children while we are still thinking and talking about the best way to create convincing lava, and what the Ring should look like as it is destroyed.

Hannah Bianchini, who had run the Visual Effects Art Department for much of the past three years, and myself were just about the last people to leave the production offices. Hannah was filing and cataloguing the huge body of work that we had accumulated, and keeping me focussed and pointed in the right direction. I was still doing work on the DVD packaging when Peter and Richard were well into development on their next projects, and one by one the different departments had emptied their offices and moved on. We had long before said goodbye to the actors who had done such a wonderful job of bringing the characters to life, and the studios in which these extraordinary films had been made were now quietly awaiting the next storm of activity.

THE GREY HAVENS

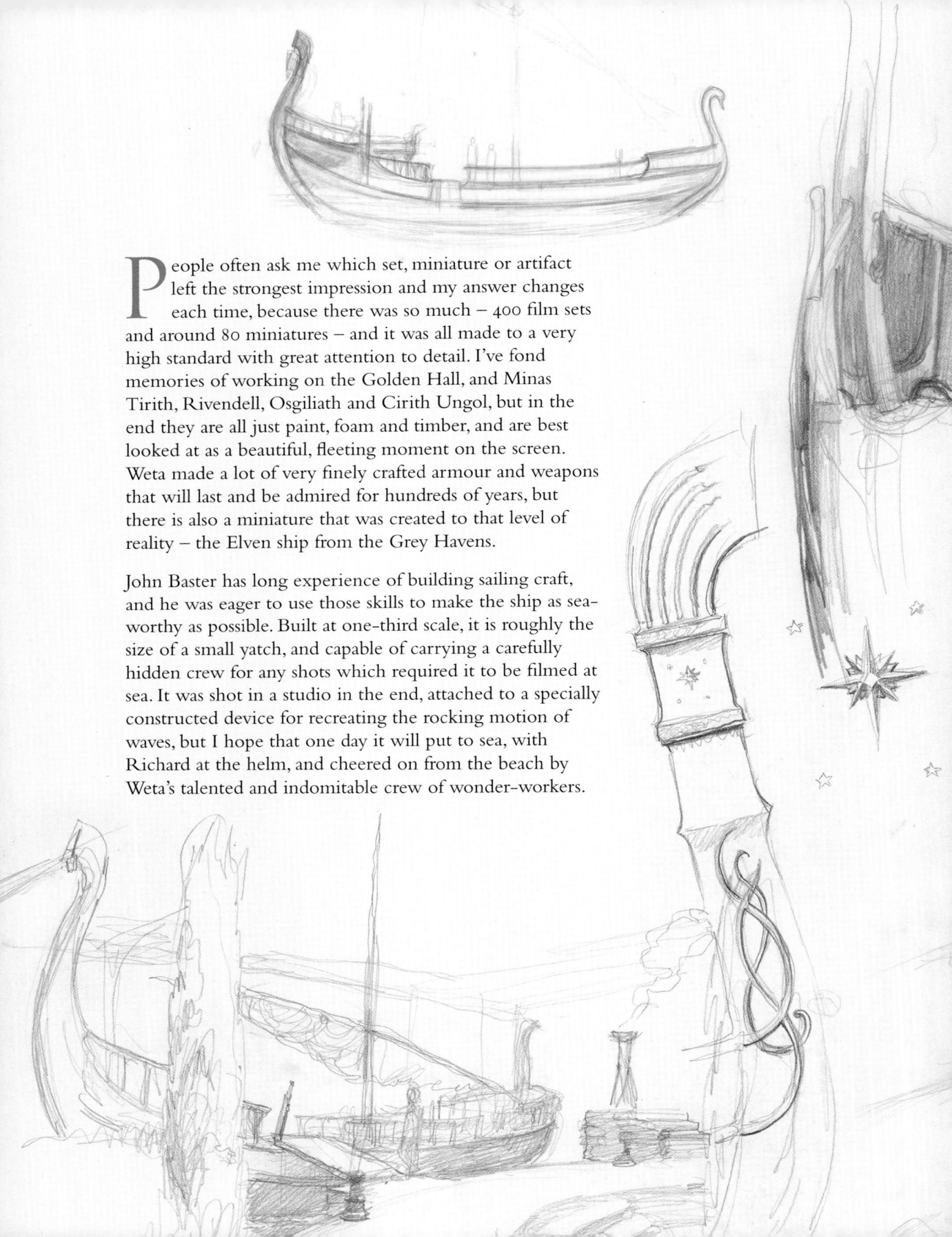

People often ask me which set, miniature or artifact left the strongest impression and my answer changes each time, because there was so much – 400 film sets and around 80 miniatures – and it was all made to a very high standard with great attention to detail. I've fond memories of working on the Golden Hall, and Minas Tirith, Rivendell, Osgiliath and Cirith Ungol, but in the end they are all just paint, foam and timber, and are best looked at as a beautiful, fleeting moment on the screen. Weta made a lot of very finely crafted armour and weapons that will last and be admired for hundreds of years, but there is also a miniature that was created to that level of reality – the Elven ship from the Grey Havens.

John Baster has long experience of building sailing craft, and he was eager to use those skills to make the ship as sea-worthy as possible. Built at one-third scale, it is roughly the size of a small yatch, and capable of carrying a carefully hidden crew for any shots which required it to be filmed at sea. It was shot in a studio in the end, attached to a specially constructed device for recreating the rocking motion of waves, but I hope that one day it will put to sea, with Richard at the helm, and cheered on from the beach by Weta's talented and indomitable crew of wonder-workers.

Acknowledgements

Alongside the fictional Fellowship, another fellowship was assembled and firmly established and another epic journey begun. It may seem obvious to make parallels between the story we were telling, and the story we were going through, but almost everyone who shared the experience of working on the films for all those years refers to it as a journey, and a life-changing episode. For many of us — 80% of the Art Department, for example — it was the first experience of working on a film production, and we were drawn together, not by the glamour of the film world — there wasn't a lot of glamour around the suburban warehouses and converted factories that formed the hub of the film industry in Wellington — but by a love for the story we were telling, and for the excitement involved in the almost impossible task of trying to film it. There were a good number of very experienced and cooler heads among the cast and crew of course. Grant Major, the Production Designer, and Dan and Chris Hennah always amazed me with the calmness with which they contemplated massive tasks and imminent deadlines, and the leadership of our producer Barrie Osborne gave us all confidence. Richard Taylor is the epitome of the adventurous and enterprising Kiwi, coming up with a flow of creative and ingenious solutions to film-making problems. And Peter Jackson? Well, he has been making films since he was nine.

However, I believe that most of us, even some of those I've just mentioned, were not capable of achieving what we did at the very start of the process; we had to very rapidly become capable, and overcome our limitations in order to even stay abreast of the task.

My own limitations could be characterised as a lack of the will to turn dreams into ambitions, and on into realities, and a preference for perfecting an initial impulse, rather than exploring a wide range of ideas. Both of these flaws disappeared with barely a squeak in the feverish creative atmosphere that boils around Peter and Richard when they are in full flow at Weta. And with John Howe's presence the furnace was burning even more strongly — even with the occasional ladle full of cold water that he would pour onto anything even slightly inauthentic. Over the following six years I did around 2,500 drawings, exploring every aspect of Middle-earth, hundreds of pieces of digitally created artwork as designs for effects shots — another necessary transition, but one that I've very much enjoyed — and a lot of graphic work as well, which is something I'd barely touched on before; designs for the film titles, DVD packaging; and a lot of playing around with some of the raw materials of film-making in New Zealand — paint, Plasticine and polystyrene. It was frequently exhausting, often hilarious, but always exciting and I consider it a wonderful privilege to have been able to not only illustrate one of the world's finest books, but then work on three of the best films ever made.

If I had ever had any qualms about the prospect of seeing *The Lord of the Rings* adapted for the screen, those doubts would have been swept aside by the large numbers of enthusiastic new readers that have come to the books as a result. In spite of my over-exposure to the story during the past few years, I still find the text moving, beautiful and exciting, and I know that I will continue to be inspired by it, and find fresh things in it to enjoy.

I would like to thank Jane Johnson, David Brawn and Chris Smith of Harper Collins for their friendship, wise counsel and patronage over the years, the Tolkien Estate for permission to illustrate the books, Gary Day-Ellison and Terence Caven for the design and production of this one, Ian McKellen for his Foreword – and all the actors who brought such a high level of skill and commitment to their realisations of the characters in the story.

I'd also like to thank Hannah Bianchini, Jacqui Allen, Marion Davey, Roxanne Gajadhar, and Brenna Townend who have all attempted to organise me over the last six years; my generous, talented and easy-going colleagues, Grant Major, Dan Hennah, Chris Hennah, John Howe, Nick Weir, Phil Ivey, Tanea Chapman, Jeremy Bennett, Gus Hunter, Paul Lasaine, Gareth Jensen, Adam Ellis, Daniel Reeve; Richard Taylor, Tania Rodger, and the Weta designers: Daniel Falconer, Ben Wootten, Warren Mahy, Sacha Lees, Jamie Beswarick, Christian Rivers, Shaun Bolton, Michael Asquith, Bill Hunt, Ben Hawker, Gino Acevedo, John Baster and Mary MacLachlan. I'd also like to thank the Art Department sculptors, who were such a pleasure to work with: Brigitte Wuest, Natalie Staniforth, Heather Kilgour, Kirk Nichols, Gary Hunt, Andrew Moyes, my daughter Virginia, and the prodigiously gifted and energetic Sam Genet and Ra Vincent. Draughtspeople: Helen Strevens, Tim Priest, Philip Thomas, Kate Thurston, Clarke Gregory. Ed Mulholland, Norm Willerton and Mike Hefferman, who led the construction crews, Kerry Dunn and Kathryn Lim for their fine work as set-finishers, and Brian Massey, Middle-earth's gardener.

I'd like to mention my friends in the Miniatures film unit, which was shooting – with barely a break – for years: Alex Funke, Marty Walsh, Paul Van Ommen, Belindalee Hope, Chuck Schuman, Simon Greenway and Bruce McNaught, as well as Costume Designer Ngila Dickson, and jeweller Jasmine Watson; Andrew Lesnie, John Mahaffie, Allen Guilford, Simon Raby, Richard Bluck, Alun Bollinger, for putting a final coat of fine cinematography on the sets, and Carolynne Cunningham, Liz Tan, Dave Norris and Marc Ashton for their gentle lessons in set etiquette.

Thanks also to my patient guides around the Hades of the digital realm: Joe Letteri, Jim Rygiel, Dean Wright, Libby Hazell, Aaron Cowan; Brian Van't Hul, Eric Saindon, Randy Cook, Matt Aitken, Gray Horsefeld, Eileen Moran, Annette Wullems and Suzanne Labrie; matte painters Max Dennison, Roger Kupelian, Yannick Dusseault, Dylan Cole, Karen deJong and Ronn Brown; the editorial team of Jamie Selkirk, Jenny Vial, Jo Priest, Annie Collins, Peter Skarratt; and to everyone who worked so hard on post-production.

I could go on to mention several hundred others, but I'd hate to run out of space before thanking Peter Jackson, Fran Walsh and Philippa Boyens – whose understanding of the text, and of the possibilities of cinema, made the films literate, moving and spectacularly exciting – for inviting me to join the adventure, Barrie Osborne, Rick Porras, Elena Azoula, Janine Aberry, Jan Blenkin, Matthew Dravitzki, Tanya Buchanan, for making sure that I had my ticket, New Line Cinema for paying for it, and our extended Fellowship – Susie Lee, Joe Yamamoto, Michael Pellerin, Michael Mulvihill, Mike Murphy, Kazandra Bonner, Jean-Paul Leonard, Adrianna Krikl, Par Larsson and Laura Abele, along with Lauren Ritchie, Mark Ordesky and Erin O'Donnell.

...And you, dear reader.